"The marr

Marriage. Was he crazy?

"The ceremony's Friday at four o'clock."

He *was* crazy!

"I don't want to ruin this for you," Devon snapped, "but you've left out one minor detail, Ryan. Me! Marriage takes two, and I am one of the principal parties in this lunatic scheme, or had you overlooked that?"

"How could I possibly overlook it? It's not every day a man has his bride handpicked for him."

"Stop calling me that," Devon said fiercely. "I am *not* your bride!"

"Not yet you aren't. But you will be, come Friday afternoon."

FROM HERE TO PATERNITY—romances that feature fantastic men who *eventually* make fabulous fathers. Some seek paternity, some have it thrust upon them, all will make it—whether they like it, or not!

SANDRA MARTON is the author of more than thirty romance novels. Readers around the world love her strong, passionate heroes and determined, spirited heroines. When she's not writing, Sandra likes to hike, read, explore out-of-the-way restaurants and travel to faraway places. The mother of two grown sons, Sandra lives with her husband in a sun-filled house in a quiet corner of Connecticut, where she alternates between extravagant bouts of gourmet cooking and take-out pizza. Sandra loves to hear from her readers. You can write to her (SASE) at P.O. Box 295, Storrs, Connecticut 06268.

SANDRA MARTON

A Proper Wife

Harlequin Books

TORONTO • NEW YORK • LONDON
AMSTERDAM • PARIS • SYDNEY • HAMBURG
STOCKHOLM • ATHENS • TOKYO • MILAN
MADRID • WARSAW • BUDAPEST • AUCKLAND

ISBN 0-373-11860-0

A PROPER WIFE

First North American Publication 1997.

CHAPTER ONE

HER hair was the pale gold of summer wheat, her eyes the deep purple of wood violets. And for one heart-stopping instant as she started down the steps, Ryan Kincaid thought she might not be wearing anything beneath the ankle-length, crimson velvet cape but her own honeyed skin.

Logic told him otherwise. Montano's might be New York's trendiest department store, but, he thought wryly, it didn't go in for nude modeling.

It was the way she held the cape closed that made for the incredible illusion. Her hands clutched the high mandarin collar against her chin so that the cape flared open at each stride, revealing an incredible length of elegant, curvaceous leg.

Ryan's green eyes narrowed in appreciation. She really was stunning. And she knew it. You could see it in the proud way she held herself, in the look of disdain etched on her perfect face. All the other models had smiled at the crowd of shoppers gathered at the foot of the mezzanine steps, but she moved like a queen, never deigning to notice the peasants.

It only made her all the more appealing, Ryan thought, and he felt his body stir with interest.

Getting trapped in Montano's crowded aisles during what had turned out to be the store's Friday Fashion Show was turning out to be more pleasant than he'd expected.

Frank, standing just behind him, gave a choked groan.

"Oh, me, oh, my," he whispered, "will you look at the blonde?" He gave an exaggerated sigh. "The answer to a man's dreams."

Ryan grinned. "X-rated dreams," he said softly.

It was amazing, the series of images that were flashing through his mind. And that was weird. He was not a man given to sexual fantasies: there'd always been enough beautiful women in his life to keep him more than happy with reality. But just looking at this one as she came down the mezzanine steps was putting his brain into overdrive.

"No offense," Frank murmured, "but I'd sure rather have a drink with her than with you."

Ryan smiled. "Forget the drink. I'd rather take her home, peel off that velvet cape and make a career of finding out what's underneath it."

The comment had been meant for no ears but Frank's, but just as Ryan began to speak, the music that had been playing gave an electronic burp and died. The hum of the crowd subsided.

And Ryan's words were clear and distinct in the ensuing silence.

The blonde froze.

The crowd gave a delighted gasp.

Ryan gave a soft groan of embarrassment.

What now? he thought. Did he grin? Shrug his shoulders, laugh the whole thing off? Should he offer an apology?

In the end, there were no options. The blonde's jaw tightened, her spine stiffened, and she resumed her walk down the stairs but with a purposeful stride.

A girl broke from the little cluster of models gathered at the foot of the staircase, said something and reached out a hand, but the blonde shrugged it off and marched toward him.

Frank gave a soft laugh. *"Adiós, muchacho,"* he murmured, and stepped back.

She came to a stop in front of Ryan, her beautiful face white with barely repressed rage, her eyes locked on his. He cleared his throat, then gave her the smile that had charmed some of the most exquisite women in Manhattan.

"Amazing, the tricks acoustics can play," he said pleasantly.

She said nothing, just went on looking at him with that glint of fury in her eyes.

Ryan cleared his throat again. "Listen," he said, "I'm really sorry about that, but—"

"You," she said coldly, "have the manners of a goat."

Someone in the crowd tittered. Ryan felt an unaccustomed flush of color rise into his face.

"Yes. Well, I—"

She came a step closer. A faint scent of perfume—Opium? L'Air du Temps?—teased his nostrils.

"Or are you just a pluperfect jackass?"

The titters came again, louder and more widespread. Ryan had to work at keeping his smile plastered to his face.

"Look, miss," he said, "I'm sorry if—"

"You're not the least bit sorry!" Her eyes—almost black with anger—flashed with accusation. "Why would you be? You and your kind think you can insult anyone who has to work for a living, don't you?''

"Lady," he said patiently, "don't you think you're overreacting? I'm trying to apologize but—''

She laughed coldly, showing small, perfect white teeth. "A goat could no more manage an apology than a baboon could learn the minuet!''

Giggles of appreciation swept through the crowd behind him. His face darkened and he stepped closer to her. She was tall for a woman but at six-two, he was taller; it gave him a grim kind of pleasure to see that his size intimidated her enough to make her take a quick step back.

"You're right," he said silkily, "I'm not in the least bit sorry. I enjoyed the show.''

There was a faint burst of applause, punctuated by a soft wolf whistle. Ryan turned and shot the crowd a quick smile.

The nerve of the man! Devon felt her cheeks flame as she stared up at the egotistical brute with the sea-green eyes, the black-as-midnight hair, and the smirk. Every eye in the place was on her now.

If only she'd ignored what he'd said.

If only she'd listened to the model who'd tried to stop her from flying at him.

If only she hadn't let Mr. Deauville drag her out from behind the counter in Fragrances minutes ago.

The manager had been breathless, his little eyes shiny with distress.

The weekly fashion show was beginning in five minutes, he'd said, while he hustled her up to the mezzanine. One of the models had been taken ill.

Devon was tall, she was slender—she would have to fill in.

Devon had tried to tell him that it was out of the question. She'd been hired two days ago to sell perfume, not to model.

But telling him anything at all had proven impossible. There'd been people and confusion everywhere. She'd still been sputtering when Mr. Deauville had shoved her into a blocked-off dressing room.

"Here's your extra girl," he'd said, and then somebody named Clyde with a lisp, a flutey voice, and the determination of a bull terrier, had grabbed her and told her to get out of her navy suit and white silk blouse and into the dress he'd shoved at her. Finally, he'd draped a velvet cape over her shoulders. It was in a color that made it about as unobtrusive as a fire engine but she'd clutched it as Clyde shoved her out the door because at least it hid the rest of her, which was crammed into a dress that covered damn near nothing.

The next thing she'd known, she'd found herself standing at the top of the stairs with a bunch of strangers peering up at her.

"It'll be OK, kid," the same model who'd tried to stop her a couple of minutes ago had said.

And it almost had been, until this...this Neanderthal, this jerk with the kind of dangerous good looks that probably made stupid women keel over, had decided to take some cheap shots at her expense.

And she, like a fool, had let his snide remarks get under her skin, launched herself at him like a missile gone haywire—

"Well?"

Devon blinked. He was looking down at her with that disgustingly masculine smirk on his face.

"Well, what?"

"Am I forgiven?" he said with a rakish smile.

"Come on, lady," a male voice called out, "tell the guy you accept his apology!"

"Yeah," another voice said, "tell him it's OK."

The man with the green eyes grinned. "You hear them," he said softly. "Come on, love. Let's kiss and make up."

He reached out, cupped her chin in his hand, and bent toward her, his eyes on hers, that damnable smile still on his handsome face. He had to be joking, Devon thought desperately, he had to be....

She looked into his eyes and saw that he wasn't.

Without hesitation, she jerked back, balled her hand into a fist, and slugged him, right in the jaw.

Holy hell, Ryan thought.

He staggered back, shaking his head against the sudden buzzing in his ears.

"Ryan?"

He blinked.

"Ryan? Are you OK?" Frank's hands closed on his shoulders. "Dammit, say something!"

Ryan touched his hand gingerly to his jaw. "She hit me," he said in wonder.

Frank began to grin. "I'll say."

Ryan's eyes narrowed. "OK," he said. "OK, I've had enough." He pulled away from Frank and turned toward the girl, who hadn't moved. "That's it," he said grimly. "I've tried to apologize but you wouldn't accept that. I admitted I behaved like a jerk and *that* wasn't good enough, either. But if you think I'll let you get away with slugging me, you've got another—''

"I'm sorry," she whispered. "I didn't mean—"

"Miss Franklin! What is going on here?"

Devon blanched. "Mr. Deauville," she said quickly. "I—I can explain, if you'll just—"

The manager turned to Ryan. "What happened here, sir?" Ryan glanced at the girl again. Her face was white as paper, her eyes huge and dark. Hell, he thought again, and he blew out his breath.

"Nothing happened," he said.

The little man's jaw tightened. "Sir, I appreciate your chivalry, but if Montano's is to maintain employee discipline—"

"And I appreciate your concern," Ryan said. His smile was polite. "But really, nothing happened. This young lady and I had a misunderstanding, and—"

"She slugged him," a delighted voice called out.

The man with the mustache turned pale. "She did what?" He whirled toward the girl, his eyes flashing. "Miss Franklin?"

Devon swallowed hard. Two weeks of pounding pavements, searching for a job; two weeks of hearing Bettina tell her what a fool she was for looking for "demeaning" work....

"It...it isn't the way it sounds," she said desperately. "If you'd just give me a moment—"

"Did you strike this gentleman or didn't you?"

"Mr. Deauville, please—"

"You're fired, Miss Franklin!"

"Wait a minute, Deauville." Ryan stepped forward, frowning. "You can't just fire her."

"Butt out," Devon snapped. She swung toward Ryan, her face flushed. "Haven't you done enough for one day? You're the cause of this fiasco, you...you stupid, hypocritical jerk!"

Ryan shook his head, wincing at the words and at the sudden ache in his jaw.

"Listen, lady, I'm doing what I can to be a gentleman here, but—"

"Why waste time trying to be anything but what you are?"

Ryan's eyes narrowed. He stared at her for a long moment and then he turned to the manager dancing attendance at his elbow.

"The girl slugged me, all right," he said tightly. "Fire her."

"I already did," the little man said. He looked at Devon, his eyes cold. "I repeat, Miss Franklin, you are terminated."

Devon stared from one man to the other. Did they think she was a...a thing to be discussed as if she weren't present?

"Terminated?" she said, and gave a little laugh. In one swift, defiant motion, she shrugged the crimson cape from her shoulders and let it pool at her feet. "Take my advice, Mr. Deauville, and go terminate yourself!" Before either man could speak, she turned and walked away.

It was the longest walk of her life, up those steps and then to the dressing room. She could feel all those eyes boring into her, knowing what they saw, the dress she'd been stuffed into that was little more than a pair of thin straps and skintight black silk; the ridiculously high-heeled, black satin pumps.

But she kept her shoulders back and her head high, until, at last, she was safely inside the dressing room. Then she stripped off the dress, kicked off the shoes, put on her own clothing and whisked out the employees' door to the street.

The two cramped hotel rooms she shared with her mother just off Times Square were mercifully empty. Bettina was probably out shopping, Devon thought bitterly as she locked the door behind her, spending their last few dollars to dress herself up for tonight's visit to James Kincaid.

Devon's mouth trembled as she sank down on the edge of her sagging bed. Why had she ever agreed to go with Bettina this evening? She hadn't wanted to: last week's visit had been more than enough. The old man was just eccentric, Bettina had insisted, but Devon had felt first like a supplicant and then like a bug under a microscope.

Tonight would surely be worse. Bettina was up to something—the signs were all there. If only she'd devote half that much energy to looking for a job.

A job, Devon thought. Lord, a job!

This morning, she'd been employed. Now, barely four hours later, she wasn't.

Here she was, in a strange city, with no money and a mother who thought work was something invented for fools. And now, thanks to that insulting creep at Montano's, she was out of a job.

At least she'd gotten back some of her own. That punch had really rocked him. She couldn't believe she'd done such a thing, she, who never so much as stepped on an ant if she could help it, but he had deserved it.

A smile tilted across Devon's lips. What satisfaction there'd been in feeling her fist connect with his smug, square-jawed face.

Her smile wobbled, then disappeared.

"Damn him," she said shakily. "Damn him to hell!"

"Damn who?" Bettina said brightly, slamming the door after her.

Devon ran her hands quickly over her eyes. "Hello, Mother. I didn't hear you come in."

"I was out shopping," Bettina said, tossing packages on the bed. "I want to look my best tonight, Devon. So should you."

"I don't know why we're going at all," Devon muttered. "I don't even know why we came to this city."

"Because we have family here, that's why. And family helps family, when the chips are down."

"We have no 'family' here, and you know it."

"What a terrible mood you're in, Devon. I hope you're not going to sit around glowering tonight."

Devon took a breath. "I lost my job," she said.

"Really," Bettina said without much interest. "How do you like this dress? Too dull, do you think?"

Devon winced at the magenta silk her mother had taken from one of the boxes.

"It's . . . it's fine, Mother. Did you hear what I said? I had a run-in with a rude customer and—"

"Well, it's no loss. Selling perfume is no better than selling sweaters the way you did at Saks back home."

"Selling isn't glamorous, but it's honest work."

"Don't you dare take that holier-than-thou tone with me!" Bettina swung toward her daughter, eyes flashing. "I worked hard to support us and don't you forget it. Waiting on tables, cleaning up after people who thought they were better than me, scraping pennies to give you all the benefits so you could have the life that I'd dreamed of—and long before Gordon Kincaid came along to pay the bills, in case you've forgotten, miss."

There had been more to it than that, Devon thought savagely. There'd been an endless string of men. Uncle Harry, and Uncle John, and Uncle Phil....

"I did what I had to do," Bettina said, as if she'd read Devon's thoughts, "and it was all for you."

"I never asked for anything," Devon said tightly.

"The sacrifices," Bettina said, "the struggle..."

Devon shut her eyes. I won't listen, she told herself fiercely, I won't. She'd grown up on this litany, hearing about her mother's hardships, of how she'd all but given up her own life for her daughter's...

"Next, you'll turn your back on me, same as your father did."

The bitter accusation twisted, sharp as the blade of a knife, in Devon's heart.

"You know I'd never do that, Mother."

Bettina smiled. "Good girl!" She bent down, gave Devon a kiss that was actually a cheek-to-cheek caress, and then she looked at her watch. "Oh, look at the time! Come along, darling. Grandfather Kincaid is sending his car for us and we don't want to be late. Put on something bright and pretty, for a change. And use some of my drops in your eyes, will you? You look as if you've been crying, for heaven's sakes!''

It was better than looking as if you'd been socked in the jaw, Devon thought.

What on earth had made her think of that?

Whatever the reason, she was glad of it.

For the first time in hours, Devon smiled.

CHAPTER TWO

AT A few minutes past four every Friday afternoon, end-of-week celebrants from Wall Street's financial offices began pouring out into the streets. Lounges and bars filled up with regulars intent on getting the weekend off to a quick start.

Ryan and Frank, who had made a ritual of toasting the week's end together since their university days, snagged the last pair of empty leather stools at the mahogany bar at The Watering Hole and exchanged friendly greetings with Harry, the bartender.

"Evening, gentlemen," Harry said. "The usual?"

"Yes," Frank answered, but Ryan shook his head.

"I'll have a Coke."

"A Coke?" Frank said, lifting his eyebrows. "What's the matter, pal? Did that dame's right hook rattle your brain?"

Ryan touched his hand gingerly to his jaw. "It was a good shot," he said grumpily. "Is there a mark?"

"A little shadow, maybe, right there—"

"Ouch!" Ryan drew a sharp breath just as the bartender put an ice-filled glass and an open bottle of Coke in front of him. He took an ice cube from the glass, wrapped it in his handkerchief and held it gently against his jaw. "Maybe this will help. I don't really feel like trying to explain a lump on my jaw to my grandfather.''

"Ah," Frank said, "now I get it. No booze because you're making the long drive out to see the old man, right?"

"You've got it." Ryan waggled his jaw carefully from side to side. "Can you believe that dame? She walks around, shows off damned near everything she's got, then gets ticked off when a guy notices. Whatever happened to decorum?"

"Decorum?"

"Yes. Decorum. You know, less cleavage, less leg, less of everything on display."

Frank's brows rose just a little. "This from the man who once dated Miss November?"

True enough, Ryan thought with some surprise. When had he ever cared how much a woman showed? If she was good-looking, the more, the better.

His eyes met Frank's. "It was Miss December," he said, smiling. "Don't you remember those little bells?"

Frank chuckled. "Man, do I ever!" Frowning, he peered at Ryan's jaw. "That bruise is turning color. You'd better run up a tale Grandpa will buy."

Ryan sighed. "The hell with it. If he asks, I'll tell him the truth. He'll probably tell me the girl gave me exactly what I deserved."

"The old man hasn't changed, huh?"

"Unlike the female of the species," Ryan said with a fond smile, "my grandfather is always predictable."

So was an evening in the Kincaid house, Ryan thought as Frank excused himself and headed for the lavatory.

Drinks first, in the old-fashioned sitting room. Bourbon for Ryan, seltzer for James since he'd given up whiskey on orders of his doctors. Then Agnes Brimley, his grandfather's prune-faced housekeeper would call them into the dining room for a medically approved dinner of gritty brown rice, mushy vegetables and stringy chicken. Dessert would have the look, smell and texture of pulverized soap.

Then the old man would shut the door on both logic and the disapproving Miss Brimley, light up one of the ropy cigars that were his sole remaining vice, fix Ryan with a rheumy eye and deliver The Lecture of the Month.

The World and How Much Better it Had Been Seventy Years Ago was always the choice opener. Second would come Advice on How to Manage Kincaid, Incorporated—even though in the five years Ryan had been running the development firm his grandfather had founded, he'd built it from being an east coast success to a national conglomerate.

But those were only warm-ups to James's favorite lecture, which always began with the words, "Time is passing, my boy," and ended with the admonition that Ryan was going to be thirty-two soon and that it was time he settled down.

Ryan smiled. And he would sit through it all without more than token protest. What would the pundits of high finance make of that? Ryan Kincaid, the man *Time* magazine had dubbed The

Lone Raider, would endure the lectures for the simplest, most complex of reasons—because he loved his grandfather and his grandfather loved him, even if the old man would sooner eat nails than admit it.

His grandfather had raised him and Gordon both, after their parents' messy divorce. Now, with Gordon gone, neither Ryan nor the old man had anyone else to care about.

"So, what about Sharon?"

Ryan looked up as Frank eased himself onto the stool again.

"What about her?"

"She can't be thrilled to be without you this evening, considering how she fusses over our weekly boys' night out."

Ryan grimaced. "If it's all the same with you, I'd rather not talk about Sharon."

"Problems?"

"Well, I forgot her birthday."

"Which is why we ended up in Montano's."

"Yeah, but there's more." Ryan sighed. "I thought we understood each other. She didn't want anything permanent and neither did I. Now she's starting to talk about how all her friends are getting married and having babies."

"I hope you told her you're too young to end your life."

Ryan lifted his glass, brought it to his lips, gazed into the dark liquid and then put it down again, untouched.

"The thing of it is, I'm not."

Frank recoiled in horror. "What?"

"We're pushing middle-age, in case you hadn't noticed."

"At thirty-two?" Frank began to grin. "I get it. You're anticipating Grandpa Kincaid's lecture about Getting Married, Settling Down, and Producing Little Kincaids to comfort him in his old age."

"There are times I almost think he's right." Ryan's mouth twisted. "After all, my brother's dead, and heaven knows his marriage didn't produce any heirs."

"Yeah. That was a fiasco, wasn't it?"

"What else could it have been? Gordon got himself hitched to San Francisco's own version of Jezebel."

"Bettina Eldridge, right? I remember." Frank sighed. "Look, pal, this is America. Kingdoms are not lost because the Prince Royal has yet to take himself a bride. Tell that to the old man, why don't you?"

Ryan ran his finger along the edge of his glass. "My grandfather's gotten very old," he said softly. "Time passes, you know."

"Tying on the ball and chain won't stop the clock from ticking," Frank said bluntly, "but if you think it will, there's always Sharon."

Ryan grinned. Even back in their undergraduate days at Yale, Frank had had a way of bringing things back to basics.

"Thanks, but no thanks. Marriage just isn't man's natural state."

"I'll drink to that."

"Hell, just look at the Kincaids. My mother celebrated her fifteenth anniversary by asking my father for a divorce so she could go off and become an anthropologist. My father fell for his secretary a year later and disappeared into parts unknown. My brother married a woman who saw dollar signs whenever she looked at him..."

"Marriage sucks," Frank said agreeably.

"My grandfather's always telling me that *his* marriage was a joy, but why wouldn't it have been? The rules were simpler. My grandmother was an old-fashioned woman. Pleasant, sweet-tempered, eager to please."

Frank sighed. "That's how women were raised in those days, pal. A girl was raised to be a lady. To play piano, serve tea and embroider doilies, to bring a man his slippers and his newspaper..."

Ryan's brows lifted. "We're talking about a wife," he said gently, "not a cocker spaniel."

"And with it all," Frank said, ignoring the interruption, "she'd be gorgeous and more than willing."

An image suddenly swept into Ryan's mind. He saw the blonde from Montano's, saw himself stripping her of that velvet cape. He saw her naked under his hands, all tanned, silky skin, high, sweet breasts and gently curved hips...

Damn! Ryan reached for his glass and drank the last of the chilled Coke.

"If I could find a babe like that, I'd marry her myself," Frank said emphatically.

"Who wouldn't?" Ryan grinned, glanced at his watch, and stood up. "You're describing a proper wife. But they haven't made a model like that in years. And that's exactly what I'm going to point out to my grandfather." He took out his wallet and tossed a couple of bills on the bar. "Thanks for the talk, friend. It was just what I needed."

Frank smiled modestly. "My pleasure."

"This time when the old man launches into the Why Don't You Settle Down speech, I'll sing him a chorus of I Want a Girl Just Like the Girl that Married Dear Old Grandad. Then I'll fold my arms, sit back, and smile."

As he had since childhood, Ryan sat to James's right at the Kincaid dining room table. But tonight was nothing like those childhood dinners. It was nothing like the hideous dinners of the past several years, either.

Ryan frowned. What in hell was going on?

Prepared for the sort of awful meal he'd described to Frank, he'd come close to falling out of his chair when Miss Brimley had come marching in with the first course.

"Ah," James had said happily.

"Ah," Ryan had dutifully repeated, and prepared for the worst. But when his grandfather had uncovered the tureen, a wonderful scent had wafted to Ryan's nostrils.

"Lobster bisque?" he'd said incredulously.

"Lobster bisque," James had replied.

Agnes Brimley had glared.

The bisque had been followed by well-marbled beef, baked potatoes slathered in sour cream, and tossed green salad with Roquefort dressing.

"And a good claret to wash it all down, of course," James had said.

Now, with the meal ending, Ryan cleared his throat.

"Are we . . . celebrating something, Grandfather?" he asked carefully.

James looked up from his plate. A strange little smile skimmed across his mouth.

"I hadn't thought of it that way, my boy, but yes, I suppose you might say that we are."

Ryan nodded. "And what would it be, sir?"

James smiled and shook his head. "No more questions for now, Ryan. We'll talk after dessert, I promise."

As if on signal, Miss Brimley banged open the service door, the very briskness of her step an indication she disapproved of whatever it was she carried on the oval silver platter in her hands.

"Dessert," she said coldly.

Ryan stared at the platter as she extended it to him. He hadn't seen such an assortment of goodies since childhood. Tiny golden creampuffs, bite-size chocolate éclairs, chunky squares of shortbread....

He raised shocked eyes to Miss Brimley. "Are those white-chocolate brownies?"

She sniffed. "Indeed."

He started to reach for one, thought of the workout he put himself through each morning, and drew back his hand.

"I, ah, I don't think so, thanks."

The housekeeper's expression softened, if only slightly. "At least someone's still using his brain as God intended!"

James wheezed out a laugh. "If you are trying to ruin my appetite, Brimley," he said, helping himself to one of everything, "it will pain you to know you are not succeeding. Bring in the coffee, if you please. Real coffee, not that decaffeinated swill you've been pawning off on me all these years. Then shut the door and leave us alone."

When she'd done as ordered, James sighed, reached inside his vest, took out a cigar—an act that only recently had seemed daring but which now was all but fraught with innocence, Ryan thought dazedly—and bit off the end.

"Excellent meal, my boy, don't you think?"

Ryan rose and took his grandfather's old-fashioned cigar lighter from its place on the mantel.

"I suppose that depends on your definition of excellent," he said, his tone wry. He held out the lighter and flicked the wheel. "Julia Child would probably agree, but I suspect your doctors would take a different view."

"Doctors," James said dismissively. "Shamans, you mean, beating their drums and dancing around the fire when we all know the best they can hope to do is delay the inevitable."

Ryan grinned. "Your diet may have changed but I see your disposition is still as sweet as ever."

The old man chuckled, then drew on the cigar until the tip glowed bright red.

"So," he said, blowing out a wreath of smoke, "what's new in your life, young man?"

"Why don't you tell me what's new in yours first?"

James's lids drooped down over his eyes. "What could be? I spend my days taking pills and eating pablum."

"Not tonight."

"No." James smiled. "Not tonight."

"You said you'd explain that cholesterol-laden feast once we'd finished it."

"You don't mind if we have a chat first, do you?"

Ryan frowned. His grandfather's tone was light. Why, then, did he feel so uneasy?

"No, of course not. What would you like to talk about?"

"I told you. What's new in your life?"

"Well, let's see . . . We've decided to bid on that property in Santa Fe, and the subdivision we're developing outside Vegas will—"

"How did you get that bruise on your jaw?"

Ryan grinned. "Would you believe me if I said I bumped against the shower door, reaching down for the soap?"

"No," James said, his eyebrows lifting. "I would not. Did some irate husband give it to you?"

"Grandfather!" Ryan shook his head. "I'm surprised at you," he said, trying not to smile. "You know I believe in the sanctity of marriage."

The old man got a strange look on his face. "I'm counting on that. And I'm still waiting to hear how you came by that bruise."

"Suppose I said a woman gave it to me?"

James chuckled. "I'd say you probably more than deserved it. All right, don't tell me how it happened. I don't suppose it matters." He tapped his cigar against the rim of an ashtray. "What else is new?"

"Well, that Vegas subdivision—"

"Yes, yes," James said impatiently, "I'm sure Kincaid, Incorporated, is doing fine. You've made an enormous success of the company, more than I ever did, and we both know it."

Ryan laughed. "Wait a minute," he said. "This is too much for one evening. First that meal, then flattery—"

"I meant," James said, his voice overriding Ryan's, "what's new in your private life?"

"Ah." Ryan smiled and sat down. "We go straight to the bottom line. You want to know if I've proposed marriage to anyone between now and the last time I saw you."

"Not to 'anyone,'" his grandfather said without smiling back. "To a woman who would make a good wife."

"A *proper* wife," Ryan said, and chuckled.

"I see nothing amusing here, young man!"

"I was just thinking of a conversation I had with Frank Ross—you remember Frank, don't you, sir?"

"I do. I take it he has not settled down yet, either."

"I'm not sure you appreciate how the world has changed," Ryan said gently. "Women aren't what they were."

"They are precisely what they were. There have always been women men should marry. The trick is to find them."

"Well, when I find one—"

"When, indeed," James said sharply. "At the rate you're going, it will be never. And time is passing."

"Grandfather," Ryan said firmly, "I really have no wish to discuss this tonight."

The old man gave him a searching look. Then he sighed and stubbed out his cigar.

"This room is drafty. Let's go into the library."

Ryan rose to his feet. "Let me help you, sir," he said as James put his hands on the arms of his chair. It was an offer he made each time he saw James struggling to stand. The response was always the same. "I'm not in my grave yet," the old man would say.

But not tonight.

"Yes," his grandfather said, "I suppose you'd better."

Ryan's eyes shot to the old man's face, but it gave nothing away. He eased him to his feet, led him across the hall to the library where a fire blazed in the hearth despite the mildness of the fall evening, and settled him into a leather wing chair.

James sighed. "That's better. Now pour some cognac."

Ryan started to object, then thought better of it. Why not cognac? Compared to dinner, cognac was small change. He poured drinks, handed one snifter to his grandfather, then drew a chair to the fire and sat down.

"All right, Grandfather," he said, "let's have it."

"Have what?" James assumed an air of innocence.

Ryan's eyes narrowed. "You've pushed me as far as I'm going to go. Now I want some answers. What's going on?"

"Why are young men always so impatient?"

"Grandfather..." Ryan said, his tone a warning.

"All right, all right. I suppose you know that my eighty-seventh birthday is fast approaching."

"So you gave yourself an early gift? A meal that would make your doctors tear out their hair if they saw it?"

"This is my life, not theirs." James's eyes met his grandson's. "Do you remember any of what you learned in Sunday school, my boy?"

"Well," Ryan said carefully, "that depends."

"I'm referring to the biblical injunction that a man is entitled to live three score years and ten." James smiled. "I've done a bit better than that."

Ryan smiled, too. "You always managed to get a good return on your investments, sir."

"I went on that hideous no-fat, no-sugar, no-taste regimen seven years ago at the urging of my doctors. They convinced me that a man of eighty, who'd survived the sort of surgery that kills men half that age, might improve his lot by eating wisely if not well."

"It was good advice."

"It was—until now."

"Come on, Grandfather. You're not going to throw in the towel just because you're turning eighty-seven in a couple of months!"

"I had my semiannual checkup last week." James's tone was brisk. "The doctors suggested I make certain my affairs were all in order."

Ryan's smile faded. "What do you mean?"

"I mean that not even a diet of pap can keep a man living beyond his time—which is as it should be. No one should take up room on this overcrowded planet forever."

"That's nonsense!"

"It is absolutely logical, and you know it. And before you ask . . . yes, I have sought a second medical opinion. It confirms the first. It's time to tally up the books."

Ryan felt his gut twist. He loved his grandfather fiercely. James had been his surrogate father and his professional mentor. He'd been everything, all the family Ryan had ever known. The years had passed—of course they had. Still, in a way that had nothing to do with rational thought, he'd expected to have more time.

"There's no reason to look so bleak, boy. I've enjoyed my life. Truly, I have no regrets."

Ryan cleared his throat. "What about seeing another doctor? A specialist?"

"I told you, I already have. A battery of them. They've all muttered their magical incantations and read their chicken bones—and they're in complete agreement."

Ryan got to his feet and paced across the room. "There's got to be something you can do."

"There isn't."

"Something *I* can do, then!"

"There is."

Ryan swung around. "What? Tell me, and I'll do it."

"Will you?" James said softly. "Can I count on you to do something that may, at first glance, seem . . . difficult?"

Ryan's eyes narrowed. "Have I ever let you down, sir?"

The old man smiled. "No. No, you have not."

"Tell me what you want and I'll take care of it."

James hesitated, then cleared his throat.

"I had a visitor last week," he said. "Two visitors, actually. Your brother's widow—and his stepdaughter."

Ryan frowned at the abrupt change in topic. "Bettina came to see you?"

"Yes. With her daughter, the offspring of husband number one, Gordon's unlucky predecessor twice removed."

"But why? I mean, Gordon's been dead more than a year."

"Oh, Bettina babbled on and on about family for a while but eventually she got down to basics."

"I'll bet." Ryan's tone was harsh. "What did she want?"

"Money. Not that she said so. Whatever else she is, Bettina's not stupid. She'd never be so obvious."

"She's obvious enough. The only one who never saw through her was Gordon."

"Evidently he did, at the end."

"What do you mean?"

"He not only left Bettina, he cut her out of his will."

Ryan's eyebrows angled in surprise. "Are you serious?"

"Absolutely. He left his money to charity and his house in San Francisco to me."

"Damn," Ryan said softly. A slow grin crept over his mouth. "Now Bettina wants you to do something about it."

"What she wants, as she so delicately put it, is for me to remember that she is one of us."

"The hell she is!"

James nodded. "I agree. But there are other considerations."

"What other considerations? The woman's no good. She must have slept in a hundred different beds before she set her sights on Gordon."

"Including yours?"

Ryan swung toward James. "No," he said harshly, "not including mine—but it wasn't for lack of effort. She made that clear enough." His eyes narrowed. "How did you know?"

James smiled. "I was only seventy-nine when she married Gordon," he said wryly. "A man in his prime can always read a woman like that."

"Gordon couldn't," Ryan said, his expression still stony.

The old man sighed. "This isn't about your brother's inability to see the truth, it's about responsibility."

"Are you saying you feel sympathy for this woman?"

"I'm not talking about sympathy. I'm talking about responsibility. And family obligation. Those things are important, Ryan. Surely you know that."

Ryan looked at James's lined face, at the hand holding the cognac glass and its slight but perceptible tremor, and he forced himself to swallow his anger.

"You're right, so if you're about to tell me you've decided to deed Bettina that house in San Francisco or include her in your will, you needn't worry. What you do with your estate is your business, sir. You don't owe me any explanations."

"But you wouldn't approve."

"No. I wouldn't."

James laughed. "Direct, as always."

Ryan smiled back at the old man. "I wonder where I could possibly have picked up such a trait?"

"Believe me, my boy, I have no intention of giving Bettina anything. I'd never countermand Gordon's desires."

"Well, then, I don't see—"

"Did I mention that her daughter was with her?"

"Yes." Ryan crossed the room and poured himself some more cognac. "She must be... what? Seventeen? Eighteen? The last I saw her—the only time I saw her, come to think of it—was the evening before Gordon moved to the coast. He brought Bettina and the girl here for dinner."

"Your memory is better than mine. I didn't remember the girl at all."

"That's because there's nothing to remember. The child sat like a lump. She was a gawky-looking thing, all bones and knees, decked out in frills that didn't become her."

James smiled. "You'll be glad to hear she's improved somewhat," he said dryly.

"Well, I suppose she's past the awkward age."

"Indeed," James said, holding out his empty glass and nodding toward the cognac bottle.

Ryan looked at the glass in the old man's hand, hesitated, then gave a mental shrug. What did it matter now?

"Meaning," he said as he poured the cognac, "she's a chip off the old block?"

"Like her mother? No, not at all. They don't even look alike. The girl must take after her father. She's very fair." James smiled. "Bettina was all got up in some purple thing like a pair of Doctor Denton's, only two sizes too small and without attached feet."

Ryan laughed. "A catsuit, I think it's called."

"But the girl was dressed as if she were going to have tea with the Queen. Demure little suit, white blouse with a bow at the throat, yellow hair skinned back in a bun."

"Probably as much a costume as Bettina's," Ryan said with a shrug. "Maybe they figured you'd be an easier touch if the girl looked sweet and innocent."

"It's possible, but somehow I don't think so. The girl was very quiet. Bettina kept trying to involve her in the conversation but she just sat there, quiet as a mouse."

"Still a lump, it would seem."

"Well, Bettina certainly did all the talking. She says Gordon cut her out of his will in a fit of temper."

Ryan snorted. "She only wishes!"

"I didn't believe it, either. So after they'd left, I phoned my attorney and had him do some checking." James smiled coldly. "Cutting Bettina out had been deliberate, all right. Seems Gordon had found her in bed with some man."

Ryan finished his cognac, put down his glass, and folded his arms over his chest.

"I hope you phoned Bettina and told her that."

"I haven't told her anything, Ryan. I wanted to speak with you first. You see, my attorney learned something quite unexpected. It seems Gordon had intended to make another change in his will."

"What kind of change?"

"The week before his death, he stopped by to see his lawyer. He said he'd been thinking about the girl."

"Bettina's daughter?"

James nodded. "He said Bettina had shuttled her off to boarding school as soon as they were married because she didn't want a child underfoot and he felt guilty, not having done anything to stop it. He said he'd never paid her enough attention or fulfilled the obligations of a stepfather."

Ryan sighed. He was beginning to see the picture.

"Look, Grandfather, if you want to continue paying the girl's tuition—"

James chuckled. "She's twenty-three, Ryan. She's been out of school for four years. And I can see why Gordon was concerned about her. She's not at all like the young women one sees today. There's no hard edge to her, no sophistication. I suppose it's the boarding school that did it. It's one of those old-fashioned places that hardly exists anymore, where young women are taught to be proper ladies. According to Bettina, the girl plays piano, embroiders, even knows how to serve a proper tea."

Ryan laughed. "Maybe we should introduce her to Frank."

"This has nothing to do with Frank," the old man said sharply. "Are you paying attention to me, Ryan?"

"Certainly, sir. And she sounds...charming." She sounded either simpleminded or dull as dishwater, but there was no need to say that to his grandfather.

"At first, I was surprised Bettina would have chosen a school that emphasized such things but then I realized she'd hoped her daughter would make the right friends, perhaps meet the brother of some rich classmate and marry him."

"But she didn't?" Ryan grinned when James shook his head. "I see. She's not awkward anymore, she's just homely. Poor Bettina. Her scheme backfired."

"I wouldn't call the girl 'homely,'" James said thoughtfully. "It's just that she's without artifice. Quite proper and demure."

"Well, then," Ryan said, trying to mask his impatience, "I'm sure she'll find a good husband sooner or later."

"I'm certain of it," James said, and smiled.

"Look, Grandfather, haven't we gotten off the subject? We were discussing—ah, we were talking about—"

"My death, that's what we were discussing, and what you can do to make its approach easier. I'm getting to it, if you'll—" There was a knock at the library door. "Yes?" the old man said irritably as it opened. "What is it now, Brimley? Can't you bear to leave me in peace for a moment?"

"You have guests, sir," the housekeeper said, her voice fairly humming with disapproval.

"Is it nine o'clock already?" James sighed. "No wonder you were getting impatient, my boy. I lost track of the time. I thought we had at least another hour before Bettina and her daughter arrived."

Ryan stared at his grandfather. "What do you mean?"

"I asked them to come by this evening, after dinner."

"What in hell for?"

"So you could meet her, of course."

Ryan thrust his hand into his black hair and scraped it back from his forehead.

"Sir," he said gently, "I'm afraid you're a bit confused. I've met Bettina before, remember?"

James slapped his hands against the arms of his chair.

"Don't patronize me, boy. I am not senile. It's my body that's failing, not my brain. I am not talking about Bettina. It's Devon I want you to meet."

"Devon?"

"Don't look so blank, for heaven's sake. Yes, Devon. Bettina's daughter. Your brother's stepchild."

"But why? Look, if you want to do something for her...give her money, whatever—"

"What I want, Ryan, is that you promise to honor the request I shall make of you."

"I will. I've already told you that, sir, but what does it have to do with—what's her name?"

"Devon," the old man said. "And it has everything to do with her. You see, I've thought of a solution to all my problems."

"What problems?"

"The ones I've spent the last hour enumerating," James said testily. "Haven't you been listening? My concern that you settle down with the right wife."

"That," Ryan said with a wave of his hand.

"Yes. That. And now this other thing that's come up, your brother's wish that his stepdaughter be provided for."

"Grandfather," Ryan said patiently, "I fail to see what one thing has to do with another."

A sly smile curved across James's mouth.

"They have everything to do with each other. You need a wife and the girl needs to be taken care of." The old man chuckled. "It's quite simple, Ryan. I have found you the proper wife and I want you to marry her."

The words seemed to echo through the library. Behind him, in the fireplace, Ryan heard the pop of a damp log as the heat drew the last bit of moisture from its core.

That's how I feel, Ryan thought dazedly, as if the last bit of air were being pulled from my lungs.

"You can't be serious," he said.

"I've never been more serious. And I will remind you that you gave me your word. You will marry Devon Franklin."

Franklin? Ryan thought. His heart slammed against his ribs. *Franklin?*

"Grandfather," he said in a strangled voice, but James shifted suddenly in his chair and peered beyond Ryan, his eyes lighting with pleasure.

"Devon, my dear. Please come in. I want you to meet my grandson."

Even before Ryan turned, before he saw her, he knew.

There, standing in the doorway, was the same gorgeous, evil-tempered blonde who'd slugged him six hours earlier in Montano's.

CHAPTER THREE

RYAN had heard it said that in moments of danger, time seemed to stand still.

That had never been his experience. He liked danger: it was one of the things that had made him so successful in business. When things got dicey, when other men blinked, Ryan only felt his heartbeat quicken. And then time would seem to speed up. Events, words, gestures would clip by at a lightning-quick rate, so that afterward he'd have to sit down and sort them all out.

Now, as he confronted the demure, sweet-tempered, old-fashioned girl his grandfather had hand-selected as his bride, Ryan knew for the first time what people meant when they spoke about a moment frozen in time.

He could feel each beat of his heart, hear each breath as he drew it. He could see Bettina, standing just beyond the girl, her blood-red lips moving so slowly that the words were undecipherable.

But the most incredible part of the experience was watching the tangle of emotions pass across Devon's face. Recognition first, and then disbelief. Then shock. And finally, horror.

Whatever she had expected to find in this house tonight, he had to be her worst nightmare come true.

But she couldn't be any more stunned than he was. Devon Franklin, sitting by the fireside with an embroidery hoop in her lap? Chatting politely with the other ladies of the sewing circle before returning home to cook her husband's dinner?

Ryan almost laughed. It was easier to imagine Jack the Ripper hired to carve roasts at a dinner party.

But it was easy to see why James had been fooled. The girl was a chameleon. She could take on whatever coloration she needed. At Montano's, she'd been the portrait of sexy sophistication: blond hair loose and flowing, eyes ringed with kohl, long legs flashing seductively beneath the ankle-length, velvet cape.

Tonight she looked as chaste as a nun ready to take her vows. Her silky hair was bundled back into a loose knot, her face was scrubbed free of makeup, and her delectable body and long legs were hidden beneath a gray wool dress that hung to midcalf.

And yet, if anything, she was more beautiful than before.

Ryan's eyes narrowed. Her beauty didn't change reality. She was a woman who had learned she could get whatever she wanted by trading on her looks. It was no accident that she should turn up for a visit with an old man, pretending to be Miss Innocence.

The whole pathetic scheme was obvious. Devon Franklin had created herself to suit his grandfather's tastes. James was not just an old man, he was an old-fashioned one nearing the end of his life, he had lots of money and only one heir.

Bettina and her daughter had seen a golden opportunity and moved on it.

A surge of anger roiled Ryan's blood. It was not only a ridiculous scam, it was a cruel one to try and pull on a frail old man. Neither woman had thought, if they'd thought at all, that the old man's grandson could stop them.

And Devon, he thought grimly, had not thought about *him* at all.

He started forward, his eyes fixed to hers, relishing the look of dread that would soon replace the horror in her face....

"Ryan!"

Bettina's squeal of delight shattered the silence. She hurtled past Devon and threw herself at him, rising off her toes as she wrapped her arms around his neck.

"Oh, Ryan, how wonderful! I hoped you might be here tonight! How lovely to see you again after so many years."

Ryan clasped Bettina's forearms and set her on her feet.

"Hello, Bettina." He smiled tightly as he took in the flushed, artfully made-up face, the hennaed curls, the lush body verging on ripeness. "It has been a long time, hasn't it? But I can see you haven't changed at all."

Bettina giggled. "It's sweet of you to say so." Her hand went to her hair; she patted it into place as she looked at James. "Hello, Grandfather Kincaid. You're looking well."

"I'm still breathing, if that's what you mean."

Bettina giggled again. "Such a charming sense of humor," she said gaily. She swung around and held her hand out to her daughter. "Come and give your grandpa a kiss, darling."

Ryan watched with grim pleasure as the girl took a minute to pull herself together. Then she squared her shoulders and stepped into the center of the room.

Did she think she could bluff it out?

"Good evening, Mr. Kincaid," she said. Her voice was softer than Ryan remembered it, but then, it would have to be, to suit the role she was playing. "Thank you for inviting us this evening."

"Nonsense, darling." Bettina's smile was as bright as neon. "There's no need to be so formal with your grandfather."

Ryan saw something flash in the girl's eyes. "He isn't my grandfather, Mother."

"Why, Devon. Don't be so silly. Of course he is."

"Mother..."

Devon's voice was low but there seemed to be a thread of warning in it. Ryan's eyes narrowed. The game was getting interesting.

"Leave the girl alone, Bettina. She can address me however she likes." James smiled and held out his hand. "Come here, girl, and let me see you."

Ryan's mouth thinned. Was that the plan? To contrast Bettina's avarice with the girl's modesty?

He almost smiled. It was clever, but it didn't fool him.

Devon looked at James's outstretched hand. She wanted to look anywhere but at the man she now knew was Ryan Kincaid.

Damn, she thought, it's not possible!

Bettina had not shut up from the instant they'd gotten into the Kincaid limousine. She'd rattled on and on about how much James Kincaid had liked Devon. She'd talked about how he'd never had a daughter or a granddaughter. And, oh, she'd said, she just knew how impressed he'd been with Devon when he'd had them to dinner the previous week; he'd never taken his eyes off her.

Devon hadn't replied and eventually Bettina had changed the subject. Perhaps Ryan would be there tonight, she'd said, and sighed girlishly. Did Devon remember him? He'd been at the old man's house the night Gordon had brought them there for dinner.

Devon had said she didn't and let it go at that. What was the point in adding that all she could remember of that night was wishing the floor beneath the dining room table would open and swallow her whole? It had been horrible, hearing the contempt in the old man's voice each time he spoke to Bettina; it had been even more horrible, watching her mother crawl.

And then there'd been Gordon's younger brother who'd come in late, left early, and never so much as looked at her in between.

Ryan, his name was, and Bettina had babbled on and on about him all the way here tonight, about his good looks and his money and his bachelor eligibility.

"Devon!"

She looked up. Bettina was staring at her, her eyes shooting sparks, her smile fixed and feral.

"Grandfather Kincaid is waiting," she said sharply.

Devon swallowed and started forward. Ryan was standing in her way; she expected him to move but he just stood there like a rock, his eyes cold and flat as green glass, so that she had to brush past him, her shoulder and hip feathering against his.

"It's...it's nice to see you again, Mr. Kincaid," she said, and gave James her hand.

"Such cold hands, girl." James chuckled. "What is it they say, Ryan? Cold hands, warm heart?"

"Something like that," Ryan said.

Devon looked up. She saw the faint smile on his handsome mouth, the chill in his eyes, and she stiffened. It was time for someone to make the first move, and it might as well be she.

"Good evening, Mr. Kincaid," she said. Her voice was steady, though her heart was thumping. "What an unpleasant surprise."

It was like throwing a bucket of water on a red-hot stove. There was an instant's silence, and then, with a hiss like supercharged steam, Bettina swung toward Devon, eyes wide.

"What did you say?"

It was Ryan who answered, his voice icy.

"She said that we've met before. Isn't that right, Miss Franklin?"

"We certainly have. We met this afternoon, at Montano's."

Bettina gave a nervous laugh. "I don't understand. Devon, you naughty girl, you never said—"

"I didn't know. We weren't formally introduced." Devon's smile was rimmed with frost. "I had no idea this—gentleman—was Ryan Kincaid."

Bettina looked from Ryan to Devon. "You mean, you sold something to Ryan today, at Montano's?"

Ryan gave a harsh, cold bark of laughter. Devon shot him a furious look, then turned toward Bettina.

"No, Mother. I didn't sell Mr. Kincaid anything."

James cleared his throat. "Ryan? I'm afraid I'm lost here, too. How do you and Devon know each other?"

Ryan smiled thinly. "I went into Montano's today. Miss Franklin works there. Isn't that right, Miss Franklin?"

"I worked there until this afternoon," Devon said defiantly. "I was fired."

"How unfortunate." Ryan smiled and leaned back against the edge of his grandfather's desk. "Why not tell us about it?"

Devon felt color rush into her cheeks. Damn Ryan Kincaid! Hadn't he embarrassed her enough today?

"Miss Franklin?" His voice was silky. "We're all waiting to hear the details. I'm sure it's a fascinating story."

He smiled, folded his arms over his chest and rocked back just a little on his heels. That was just how he'd looked at Montano's, that smug, superior smile curling across his too handsome face, that arms-folded, back-on-his-heels stance that said he was far too good for the rest of the world and especially for mere peons like her.

Devon drew a deep, deep breath.

"It's not fascinating," she said, "it's depressing. To think that a . . . a male chauvinist pig like *you* could—"

"Devon!"

"It's the truth, Mother," Devon said furiously, "and I'm not going to pretty things up just so we don't offend the Kincaids!"

"The truth is never offensive," James said mildly. "Why don't you tell us what happened, girl?"

Devon spun toward him. "I'll tell you what happened," she said through her teeth. "I was doing my job and your grandson here decided to make an ass of himself, that's what happened!" She flung back her head, crossed her arms over her breasts, and glared at Ryan. "And when I refused to let him insult me, I was fired."

Ryan smiled thinly. "It's amazing, how a few details left out of a story can change it so completely."

"The only detail I've left out is my full opinion of you," Devon retorted, "but I'll keep that much to myself." Her eyes glittered. "I wouldn't want to shock your grandfather."

"How generous of you," Ryan said.

"Listen, you... you—"

"Careful, sweetheart. Watch your language, or you'll blow the Miss Innocent image completely." He smiled with malice. "Actually, I think you already have. It's probably too late to salvage anything now."

"Devon?" Bettina, her knuckles white as she clenched the back of a chair, stared at her daughter. "What on earth is he talking about?"

Devon gave Ryan one last glare, then swung toward her mother.

"He's talking lies," she snapped. "I told you, I was at work—"

"She was coming down the steps in an ankle-length, velvet cape," Ryan said coldly, "looking like every man's dream, and I said—"

"A velvet cape?" Bettina blinked. "You, in a velvet cape?"

Devon flushed. "Montano's does an end-of-week fashion show Fridays. One of the girls took sick and the store manager dragged me out from the perfume counter—"

"Dragged her," Ryan said sarcastically, "tossed her over his shoulder, stripped off her clothes, stuffed her into six inches of black silk and covered the concoction with six yards of velvet." He shook his head sadly. "Really, Devon, you ought to report the guy to the Department of Labor."

"—dragged me out from behind the counter," Devon said through her teeth, "shoved me into the models' dressing room, and the next thing I knew I was going down the steps from the mezzanine, modeling this crimson velvet cape."

"Crimson," Bettina whispered. "It must have looked lovely with your coloring."

"And then this...this man said something awful and I heard it. Everybody heard it! So I went over to tell him he ought to get his brain washed out with soap and...and one thing led to another, and—"

"She said..." Ryan said pleasantly, turning to James, "that I was a goat. A jackass. A baboon. And a caveman—or was it a Neanderthal?" He shrugged his shoulders. "I really can't remember."

"I said he had no manners, and I was right," Devon snapped. "And then...then the crowd got into it. People laughed, and...and—"

"And I tried to apologize," Ryan said with an innocent smile.

Devon slammed her hands on her hips. "He tried to kiss me," she said, her lips curling.

"It was a joke."

"Some joke!"

"Yes, well, apparently Miss Franklin doesn't have a sense of humor, Grandfather." Ryan lifted his hand to his jaw and gently touched the faint purple smudge. "Because that was when she slugged me."

There was complete silence in the room. Then, like the distant wail of a siren, Bettina sobbed out Devon's name.

"Devon," she said. "Oh, Devon, you didn't!"

Ryan kept his eyes on his grandfather.

"Did you hear what I said? Your sweet-tempered, old-fashioned, demure, well-mannered gem of deportment hit me with a right hook to the jaw that would have put George Foreman to shame."

Something that was impossible to read flickered in James's eyes.

"Interesting," he said calmly.

Ryan nodded. "I thought you might think so."

"Devon," Bettina said in a hushed whisper, "how could you?"

Lord, Devon thought, how different the story sounded coming from Ryan Kincaid's mouth.

"It wasn't like that! If you'd heard him—if you'd seen him..." Devon looked wildly at the three people facing her. Bettina was staring at her in horror; James was looking at her with no expression at all. Ryan, damn him, was smirking. "I just wish I'd hit him harder!"

Bettina rushed toward Devon and flung an arm around her shoulders.

"It's the stress she's been under, my poor baby! She's spent her life among people of a certain class, and now—"

"Don't make excuses for me," Devon said angrily.

"And now, through a quirk of fate, she's been forced to associate with riffraff! Oh, what terrible times these are, that my Devon should have had to take a job as a salesclerk to put food on the table!"

Devon stared at her mother. That was nonsense! She'd been working as a salesclerk for three years, supporting herself in the tiny apartment she shared with another girl. It had been the only job she could get; the boarding school Bettina had insisted on sending her to had specialized in preparing its graduates for a silly, boring world that no longer existed.

"No," Devon said, "that isn't—"

"She should never have had to take such a menial position," Bettina said, her voice quavering. "It's just that our financial situation is so desperate. Oh, if only darling Gordon hadn't left us so unexpectedly. We all know how he was, always leaving things till the last minute." Despite her soulful expression, she couldn't keep a sudden hard glitter from her eyes. "For instance, he told me a dozen times how he planned to change the deed to our house so it was in my name and not his, but he never got around to it."

Ryan shot a triumphant look at James. There it was, the reason for Bettina's sudden appearance. She wanted the house; Devon was to have provided the distraction that would secure it for her.

He brought his hands together in slow, exaggerated applause.

"*Brava*, Bettina. What a performance! Worthy of the Broadway theater at its best."

That was precisely what Devon had been thinking, but hearing Ryan say it was quite different. Her eyes flashed him a warning as she broke away from Bettina's encircling arm.

"And you should have been taught some manners when you were little! Stop insulting people, dammit!"

"Enough," James said, his voice sharp with authority. "All of you, calm down and we can talk like reasonable people."

Bettina snapped open her purse, drew out a lace handkerchief, and dabbed it gently at her eyes.

"I should hope so," she said in a tremulous whisper. "Ryan, that was cruel."

"Nonsense." James's tone was brusque. "It's the plain truth. Gordon's actions were quite deliberate. He meant to cut you off without a cent, and he did."

"We had a teeny misunderstanding, that's all. He'd have changed his will again if he'd only had the chance. Gordon adored me. He'd never have wanted me penniless. And he'd certainly not have wanted me to give up the home we so happily shared together."

"Perhaps," James said, ignoring Ryan's snort of disgust, "and perhaps not. The only thing I know for certain is that my grandson died before he could make provision for Devon."

"For me?" Devon said, startled.

Bettina dug a sharp elbow into Devon's ribs. "I'm not surprised to hear it. Whatever problems Gordon and I might have had," she said, blithely changing tactics, "Gordon loved Devon as if she'd been his own child."

Devon saw Ryan looking at Bettina as if he expected her nose to start growing like Pinocchio's. It was hard to blame him. Her stepfather had seemed to be a decent man but she'd hardly known him. She'd spent her summers in camp, once Bettina had Gordon's money to pay for it, and only come home for Christmas and Easter.

"Gordon wanted his little girl to have the best," Bettina sighed, dabbing at her eyes with the hankie. "It would pain him terribly if he knew she was living in poverty."

"Mother, I'm not—"

"Hush, Devon." Bettina's smile was sweet but her eyes snapped with warning. "Let Grandfather Kincaid finish what he was about to say."

James cleared his throat. "It seems that one of my grandson's last expressed desires was to see Devon properly cared for."

Bettina beamed happily. "How nice."

"In fact, Ryan and I were discussing that very topic when you arrived."

"What topic?" Devon said. "You mean you were talking about me?"

James nodded. "Yes. We were formulating a plan for your future, weren't we, Ryan?"

Ryan, who had almost forgotten James's shocking "last request," remembered it now and frowned.

"A nonsensical plan," he said, "don't you agree, Grandfather?"

James smiled. "Are you sure of that, my boy?"

"I damned well am! And you should be, too, now that you've been treated to this display of sweetness and charm!"

Devon put her hands on her hips and glared from one man to the other.

"What's going on here? You can't discuss me as if I weren't even in the room!"

Ryan ignored her. "I would prefer we continue this discussion in private, Grandfather."

James nodded. "I concur."

"That's it!" Devon's chin tilted up at a proud angle. "I've had enough."

"Devon," Bettina whispered harshly, "don't be a fool!"

"Goodnight, Mr. Kincaid. I'd thank you for your hospitality but I don't really think there was any to thank you for. Mother, I'll wait for you outside."

Without a glance in Ryan's direction, Devon strode past Bettina, never pausing until she reached the privacy of the musty foyer. There, she fell back against the wall and took a deep, sobbing breath.

What a horrible scene! The old man, watching her with those unblinking eyes; Bettina, spewing those phony tears and even phonier stories of familial bliss. And Ryan Kincaid, commenting on her as if she were a commodity. The louse. The arrogant, insensitive bastard—

She cried out in shock as a pair of hard, merciless hands fell on her shoulders.

"Just where in hell do you think you're going?" Ryan snarled as he turned her toward him.

"Anyplace where I don't have to see a Kincaid face," Devon said furiously. "Let go of me!"

"That was one hell of a performance you just gave, sweetheart." Ryan's face was harsh, his eyes chill. "You're almost as good an actress as your mama."

"I—said—let—go!"

"The righteous indignation," he growled, his hands tightening as she struggled to twist free. "The outraged innocence—"

"Let go, dammit! You've no right to—"

"I've every right. You can't really think I'm going to let you and your mother pull this swindle on a sick old man!"

"I don't want anything from your grandfather. Not one miserable thing!"

"Of course, you don't," Ryan said with chill sarcasm. "That's why you're dressed like Miss Prim, why you spoon-fed him all that crap about what a well-educated, well-bred little girl you are."

"I didn't tell him anything."

"No. You let Bettina do it, while you just sat there looking as if butter wouldn't melt in your mouth."

"Listen, Mr. Kincaid, I don't like you any more than you like me, so if you'd just take your damned hands off me, I'll see to it we never have to lay eyes on each other again."

"It sounds good, baby, but we both know that your little brain is already at work, trying to figure how much you and Mama can squeeze out of Grandpa now that he told you poor, dumb Gordon wanted to see you taken care of."

"My brain is busy, all right. It's telling me that aiming for your jaw was a big mistake. I should have gone for a more sensitive part of your anatomy."

Ryan hauled her closer, his face dark with fury.

"You so much as try to hit me again, lady, and I'll... I'll— "

"You'll what?" Devon demanded, tossing her head in defiance. "Hit me back? I wouldn't put it past a louse like you!"

Ryan glared down into her angry face. Dammit, but she'd read him right! He'd never had the urge to strike a woman in his life but right now the thought of shaking Devon until her teeth rattled was almost overwhelming.

His gaze swept over her. Struggling against him had made all that pale hair come loose from its phony, godawful bun; it fell around her face like gold silk. Her eyes, even without makeup, were the purple of spring tulips. Her cheeks were streaked with pink, a shade darker than her parted lips.

Ryan's belly knotted. He couldn't recall ever being this angry—or this intrigued—by a woman in his life. The confusion made his head spin and tied his muscles in knots; it made the breath rasp in his lungs. There was only one thing he could do and he did it, pulling her, hard, against his body.

"No," she gasped, but it was too late.

His mouth was already on hers in a kiss that was as wild as it was dominating. He felt her stiffen instinctively, felt her lips tighten against his, and, just as instinctively, his mouth softened against hers and his hand slid into her hair.

Her body seemed to jerk in his arms and she made a whisper of sound.

"No," she said against his mouth, and he seized the moment and slipped his tongue between her lips.

He felt the heat of her mouth, the honeyed taste of it. Her scent—not L'Air du Temps or Opium now, but something primal and female—rose to his nostrils. She made the sound again and he recognized it for what it was, the need of a woman who wants a man, and as she rose toward him, as her arms closed around his neck and she returned his kiss, his confusion was transformed into a surge of desire.

Dammit to hell.

He thrust her from him and she fell back against the wall, her breathing as swift and erratic as his. Her dark lashes flew open, revealing those incredible violet eyes. She stared at him, her expression dazed, and it took all Ryan's strength not to pull her into his arms again.

Her hand rose slowly to her lips. She wiped the back of it across her mouth and swallowed convulsively.

"You're a horrible human being, Ryan Kincaid," she whispered.

Ryan's face was like stone. "Remember that. Maybe it'll keep you and your mother far, far away from me and from my grandfather."

He turned and walked down the hall to the library. Bettina came hurrying out just as he reached the door; she started to say something but he brushed past her without acknowledging her presence.

James, still sitting by the fire, looked up. "Interesting evening," he said mildly.

A smile twisted across Ryan's lips. "That's one way to describe it."

"Well? What did you think?"

"What I think is good riddance to bad rubbish."

"Don't mouth platitudes, boy. What do you think of the girl?"

Ryan laughed as he took the bottle of cognac and poured himself a double.

"A proper wife, you said."

"I still say it."

"We must have spent the last hour with two different Devon Franklins."

"If you're referring to the fact that she's also got some spirit—"

"She's ill-tempered, argumentative, and sharp-tongued," Ryan said, and tossed off half the cognac.

"A woman who'd roll over and play dead wouldn't keep your interest and you know it."

"She's also Bettina's daughter."

"Very astute," James said wryly.

"Come on, Grandfather, you know what I mean! Those women came to New York to try and get some money out of you."

"Bettina did. I don't think the girl is part of it. And your brother thought well of her."

"Yeah." Ryan gave a harsh laugh. "And my brother sure as hell was a terrific judge of character."

James let out a deep sigh. "I think it's time we said goodnight, Ryan. I'm feeling rather weary."

Ryan's eyes flew to his grandfather's face. Exhaustion was written across the stern old features.

"Of course, sir. I'll help you to your room."

"Brimley can help me to my room," James said testily. "Let the dragon earn her living."

Ryan smiled. "I'll send her in." He paused and cleared his throat. "I'm sorry tonight didn't go as you'd hoped," he said softly. It was a lie, but a harmless one.

"That's all right. Nothing important is ever simple, my boy. I've lived long enough to know that that is one of life's few truisms."

Moments later Ryan slid behind the wheel of his Porsche. He shook his head as he thought of how close Devon Franklin and her mother had come to catching the brass ring.

But Devon's temper had done her in.

Not that he'd really have married her. He'd walk through fire for his grandfather. But marry Devon Franklin?

Ryan shuddered as he put the car in gear. Not in this lifetime, he thought. He stepped on the gas and the Porsche roared down the driveway and into the night.

CHAPTER FOUR

MONDAY morning did not start well.

Ryan's clock radio, programmed to awaken him to soothing music at seven, instead woke him an hour later with a burst of what sounded like machine gun fire.

"...latest adventure movie, coming your way," an excited male voice screamed as Ryan, heart pounding, shot bolt upright in his bed.

He reached out a hand, slammed the radio into silence, and fought to get his bearings.

Hell, he thought, scrubbing his hands over his bristly face, waking up to that was all he'd needed. His housekeeper had done it again. In her zeal to whisk away dust, she was forever unplugging things and plugging them in again with no clue as to what small disaster she might have left behind.

Last week it had been the microwave oven, pinging away in the middle of the night; the week before, the VCR had gone on at dawn, madly recording test patterns from the local public television station.

Well, at least he was awake. Anything was better than the awful nightmare he'd been having a few minutes before.

In the dream, he'd been standing at the end of a flower-strewn aisle, not in a church but in a department store. The place was empty but for Frank, who stood beside him dressed in jeans, black bow tie, sweatshirt and sneakers.

Ryan, on the other hand, was in a tuxedo.

What are we doing here? Ryan said, tilting his head warily toward Frank's.

Frank gave him a sad smile. *You tell me, pal*, he said, and before Ryan could reply, there was a swell of music from the mezzanine and a woman in an ankle-length, crimson velvet cape suddenly materialized at the far end of the aisle.

Who's that? Ryan whispered.

Frank sighed. *How should I know? It's your dream.*

Ryan stared down the aisle, his brow furrowing. He couldn't see the woman's face—it was hidden behind an elaborate white lace veil—but there was something very familiar about her.

Slowly, she began walking toward him. The cape swung gently open at each step, revealing a stunning length of long, tanned leg.

Frank stepped back.

Wait, Ryan said, *I'm not ready for this*.

The woman glided to a halt. Her hands rose to her veil.

Wait, he said, *wait*.

It was too late.

Ryan shrieked as Agnes Brimley lifted the veil from her persimmon-sour face.

With a nervous laugh, Ryan swung his legs off the bed. He sat still, taking deep breaths.

"Damn," he muttered.

So much for gagging down Sharon's home-cooked version of chicken Marengo last night.

He'd canceled his date with her Saturday evening. The thought of dealing with her and Devon Franklin in one twenty-four-hour period had seemed more penance than anyone should have to pay for being male. But by Sunday, with his equilibrium regained, he'd decided that it was foolish to prolong things.

Their relationship was over and it was time she acknowledged it.

Experience had taught him that public places were best for goodbyes. There was less likelihood of a scene if there were strangers around. So he'd made a reservation at an Italian restaurant in midtown—a businesslike place, nothing romantic—and then he'd telephoned Sharon.

"No, no, Ryan," she'd said in a little-girl whisper she'd developed in the past week, one that he wryly suspected would have shocked the pants off the dozen stockbrokers who took orders from her. "Let's not eat out tonight. You come to my place. I'll make us something simple."

Ryan groaned and put his hand on his flat, muscled belly where Sharon's "something simple" still lay like a ball of lead. He rose to his feet, padded naked to the bathroom, opened the medicine cabinet and took out a packet of Alka-Seltzer. He waited impatiently for the tablets to dissolve in half a glass of water. Then, screwing up his face and holding his breath, he slugged the water down.

The meal hadn't been the worst of the evening.

Ryan sighed as he lathered his face with shaving soap, picked up his old-fashioned, straight-edged razor and placed the blade gently against his jaw.

"Dress casually," Sharon had said, and he had, in pressed, faded jeans, loafers, and a pale yellow cashmere sweater under a leather bomber jacket.

Promptly at eight, he'd rung the bell to her apartment.

Sharon was dressed even more casually. She flung open the door wearing a smile, a pair of high heels, and a tiny red bib apron. The rest of her clothes were conspicuous by their absence.

"Hi," she said, giving him a big, sexy grin. "Guess what's on the menu?"

Ryan knew better than to answer, but that didn't faze Sharon. She wound her arms around his neck and gave him a passionate kiss.

Gently, he extricated himself from her tentacles, said he was starved, and managed to consume some half-raw thing that quivered when she put it on his plate.

After dinner, she plopped down in his lap, guided his hand to the apron ties, and asked him to guess what was for dessert.

Ryan blanched, set her carefully on her feet, and handed her a little box.

"Happy belated birthday," he said.

The box contained a pair of sapphire and diamond earrings he'd picked up the day before in a quick stop at Cartier. It was, he'd thought, a gift that would put a polite spin on a goodbye visit.

Wrong.

His heart and his stomach sank together as he saw the light go on in Sharon's eyes. Square little jewelry boxes were not a smart thing to give a woman who was hearing wedding bells. Why hadn't he realized that?

Because of the damned Franklin girl, that was why. It was her fault. He'd started to buy Sharon an amethyst necklace but the color of the stones had reminded him of the color of Devon Franklin's eyes and he'd turned away from the necklace counter in confusion.

"Oh, Ryan," Sharon whispered, and before he could say a word, she popped open the box.

"Earrings," she said. "How—how thoughtful."

Ryan cleared his throat. "Sharon, we have to talk."

"I agree," she said, snapping the box closed. "Emily and Mark got engaged last week."

Emily and Mark? Ryan had no idea who they were, but instinct told him this wasn't the time to ask.

"That's nice," he said cautiously, "but—"

"I think it's time we did, too."

There it was. The taunting cape had been flung aside and the matador's *espada* glinted in the arena sun.

Ryan tried an impersonal smile.

"You're a lovely woman, Sharon. But when we first met, we agreed—"

"That was then," Sharon said, her voice suddenly cold.

Ryan's eyes had narrowed. "Then, now, next week... It won't change. And it's time we dealt with it."

The evening had not ended in the civilized manner he'd hoped. Sharon had called him a name. Several names, in fact, and then she'd pointed dramatically at the door.

"Get out," she'd shrieked.

And he had.

Ryan shuddered as he recalled the nasty scene. Why did women insist on changing the rules in the middle of the game? he thought as he stepped into the shower. That was the one thing a man could count on. You sure as hell couldn't count on the female of the species for consistency.

Just look at Devon Franklin. One minute she could make a man think she was the sexiest thing alive. The next she was a leading contender for Queen of the Vestal Virgins. And she was either a knowing part of her mother's scheme, or she was an innocent pawn.

He didn't know which and he didn't care. He only knew he wanted no part of her, a decision his grandfather had no choice but to accept, thanks to Devon's Friday night performance.

Ryan's jaw knotted. All he had to do now was forget he'd ever laid eyes on her.

Unfortunately, it wasn't going to be easy.

He shut his eyes as the shower beat down on him. Last night, Sharon—who was stunning, by any man's standards—had put everything she had on display. But for sheer impact, none of it had compared to Devon's slow, sexy stroll down the stairs at Montano's.

Hell, the truth was that even dressed in that prim-and-proper suit, with her hair pulled back and her face devoid of makeup, Devon had managed to stir his senses.

Ryan groaned, opened his eyes, and looked down at himself. It wasn't only his senses she'd stirred, he thought grimly.

Dammit! This had to stop.

Angrily, he jammed the shower control knob all the way to the right, shuddering at the sudden rush of icy water that spewed over him. He stood beneath it without flinching while he counted to two hundred, and then he shut the water off and stepped briskly onto the mat.

So what if he'd overslept? He was going to take the time for his morning workout anyway. An hour in his basement gym—thirty minutes on the Nautilus, thirty in the lap pool—another cold shower and whatever cobwebs were still in his head would be gone.

His stomach clenched, and he groaned and put his hand against his belly.

The effects of Sharon's chicken Marengo would, unfortunately, take a little longer to fade.

The workout turned out to be just what he'd needed.

By the time he reached the glass tower that housed Kincaid, Incorporated, on its highest six floors, Ryan's mood had considerably improved. Devon and Sharon were both memories. What was Frank doing tonight? he wondered as he rode the elevator to the fortieth floor. Maybe they could take in a game at the Garden.

The receptionist gave him her usual dazzling smile. Ryan smiled back, gave a wave of the hand to one of the mailroom clerks, and paused beside his secretary's desk.

"Good morning, Sylvia. How was your weekend?"

Sylvia looked up. "Probably better than yours," she said. "What's that on your jaw? Did somebody slug you?"

His hand shot to his face. "No," he said abruptly, "of course not. Why would you even ask such a..."

Ryan frowned. The door to his private office was standing partly open, which was unusual. His frown deepened as he caught a swift glimpse of a pair of boot-clad feet pacing across the Berber carpet.

"What the hell? Sylvia? Is somebody in my office?"

"Yes."

"Yes? What do you mean, yes? You know better than to let anyone—"

"I know sir, but I was sure this would be OK. It's your niece."

Ryan went very still. "My what?"

"Your niece." The smile fell from his secretary's middle-aged face. "Well, that's what she said, Mr. Kincaid. She said her name was Devon Kincaid and—"

"No calls for the next half hour," Ryan said sharply. He strode into his office, slammed the door shut behind him, marched to his desk and punched the off button on the telephone.

Devon, who was standing at the window, swung toward him.

"It's about time," she said tightly. "I've been waiting over an hour!"

Ryan tossed his briefcase on his desk, undid the buttons on his jacket, and glared at her.

"What are you doing here?"

"Your secretary assured me that you always got in before nine, but—"

"Never mind what my secretary assured you!" Ryan stalked toward her, anger stamped into every feature of his face. "Where do you get off, telling her your name was Kincaid and that you were my niece?"

"I am," she said, flushing slightly. "Your stepniece, if you want to get technical about it."

Ryan's eyes narrowed. "I don't want to get technical about it. I'm not even sure there *is* such a thing as a 'stepniece.'"

Although she was certainly done up to look like a niece this morning, Ryan thought furiously, assuming you got to pick your niece from the latest Ralph Lauren ad in *Vanity Fair*.

No red velvet capes today, no prim and proper suits. Devon was wearing an oatmeal-tweed blazer opened over a black turtleneck shirt, faded jeans and ankle-high leather boots. Her hair was drawn back loosely from her face, secured at the nape of her neck with a demure black bow.

Ryan's gut tightened. On second thought, she didn't look the least bit like anybody's niece. Nieces were supposed to be cute little girls in gingham dresses, but there was nothing cute about Devon. Her jeans clung to her calves and slender thighs; her high, rounded breasts pressed lightly against the black cotton shirt. And all Ryan could think about the tied-back, platinum hair was that it would only take one tug of his finger to undo the ribbon and send all that pale silk cascading over her shoulders.

Hell, he thought, and his expression grew even more stern.

"Well?" he said coldly. "I'm waiting. What's so important that you lied your way into my office?"

"I needed to see you—and I didn't think it would be such a hot idea to drop the reason on the dragon outside."

"OK," Ryan said, leaning back against his desk and folding his arms, "you're seeing me. Now, what's this all about?"

A flush rose in Devon's cheeks. "Must you always try to humiliate me? You know damned well why I'm here. You just want me to say it because you know it'll embarrass me."

"I hate to ruin this little scene for you, Devon, but I don't think it's possible to embarrass you. And I still don't know what you're talking about."

Devon stared at Ryan's implacable face. It was wrong, that a man so astonishingly good-looking should also be such a worthless bastard.

Not that his arrogance and his nastiness really surprised her. She'd spent years among people of his class; she knew what they were like. That awful boarding school might not have taught her how to type or balance a checkbook but it certainly had taught her that the rich thought they owned the world.

"Well? Are you going to tell me why you've come here, or am I going to call Security and have you escorted out?"

"You are, without any question, the most miserable son of a—"

"Such sweet talk, darling." Ryan walked around his desk, sat down in his chair, shoved it back and put his feet up on the desk. He smiled coolly.

"You're going to wind me around your finger if you keep it up."

Devon stared at him as the awful possibility that he was telling the truth began dawning. She cleared her throat.

"You . . . you really don't know why I'm here?"

"No, dammit, I don't. And you've got two minutes to tell me before I toss you out of here on your pretty little behind!"

Devon licked her lips. Just say it, she told herself, and get it over with.

"Your grandfather—James Kincaid—wants . . . he wants us to get married."

She jammed her hands into the pockets of her blazer, fisting them tightly for courage, while she waited for his reaction. Would he burst into laughter? Throw her out of his office? Send for the men in the white coats?

But he had no reaction. Oh, he looked upset. Even mildly piqued. But he certainly didn't look the way she felt, as if the entire planet had turned upside down.

"Damn," he said.

"Damn?" she said, sinking down onto the edge of a chair. "I tell you that your grandfather has decided to play matchmaker-from-hell and all you can say is 'damn'?"

"How did you find out?"

"How do you think I found out? My mother told me."

Ryan nodded. Evidently the old man had discussed his plan with Bettina before Friday night's get-together. It surprised him that James would have spoken with Bettina before speaking with him—but why should it? The real surprise was that his grandfather would have even considered such an outrageous scheme in the first place.

Thank God, James had seen Devon as she really was.

"Well?" Devon sprang to her feet. "Aren't you going to say something? Are you just going to let your grandfather and my mother go on thinking they can arrange our lives? Not that I'd ever marry you," she added quickly. "Why, I'd sooner—"

"Relax. The idea's as dead as yesterday's news."

"Dead as yesterday's..." Devon's eyes widened. "Then, you *did* know about it?"

"My grandfather may have mentioned something," Ryan answered casually. He looked at her, his eyes icy. "I told him it was out of the question."

"I should hope so!"

His teeth showed in a quick, mirthless smile. "I can just imagine how you took the news. Helping your mother get her claws into the Kincaid money is one thing, but—"

"That's a lie!"

"I'd give anything to have seen Bettina's reaction to the thought of marrying you off to me with my grandfather's blessing. She must have figured she'd hit the jackpot."

Devon flushed. Ryan's unkind assessment was right on the mark. Her mother had shrieked with excitement.

"Not at all," she said, lying through her teeth. "My mother is only interested in my happiness."

Ryan grinned. "Come on, baby, who are you kidding? The two of you probably spent the weekend planning your new life." He shook his head in a mock parody of sorrow. "Too bad my grandfather never got around to telling her the deal was off before you and she celebrated."

Devon's head came up. "What do you mean?"

"James trotted his idea past me Friday night." Ryan smiled coolly. "I turned it down before you and Bettina were out of the Kincaid driveway."

"My mother didn't know a thing about this Friday night." Her face whitened. "Your grandfather called this morning."

Ryan sat up straight in his chair. "That's impossible."

"He phoned early. Six or six-thirty, I think. I was reading through the paper, checking the want ads, when the phone rang. It was your grandfather, and he asked to speak with Bettina. And when she got off the phone, she said—she said..." Devon caught her breath. "Why are you looking at me like that?"

"I don't believe it," Ryan muttered. "How could he?"

"You've got to speak to him. Make him understand that it's out of the question."

"Of course it is." Ryan shot to his feet. "The old man must have lost his mind!"

"He has to call my mother and tell her it was all a mistake. She...she's rather excited about this, and—"

"Don't worry," Ryan said grimly. "Last time I checked, this was still a free country. People don't get married because other people want them to."

Devon felt as if a load was being lifted from her shoulders. "Excited" was a pathetic way to describe Bettina's reaction to James's call. "Frenzied" was far more accurate.

"Of course not. I just— I want to be sure your grandfather understands that . . . that—"

"Oh, I'll make sure he understands," Ryan said tersely. "He's got this sudden fixation. But he's not a fool, Devon. I'll explain very clearly that I wouldn't marry you under any circumstances."

"Just be sure he knows I feel exactly the same way," she said, her voice brisk.

Ryan's green gaze darkened as it skimmed over her, lingering on the swift rise and fall of her breasts before returning to her face.

"On the other hand," he said with a little smile, "I wouldn't pass up the chance to take you to bed."

Devon's hand flew up but he caught it easily in his.

"If you're honest," he murmured, "you'll admit you've thought the same thing."

"Never!"

Ryan's hand threaded into her hair, fisting in its abundance, forcing her head back so that her beautiful, treacherous face was turned up to his.

"We'd be like a Fourth of July fireworks and you know it. Starbursts and flames and rockets to the moon."

"What an incredible ego you have! I just told you, I'd never—"

"You would. Hell, you almost did, right there in the foyer of James's house the other night. All I had to do was lift your skirt and you'd have wrapped those long legs around me, begged me to—"

This time when she tried to hit him, he was ready. He laughed, forced her face to his, and kissed her.

"Stop it," Devon gasped, tearing her mouth from his.

Ryan put his arms around her. "Is that really what you want?" He looked into her eyes as he brought his lips to hers again.

But there was nothing demanding in his kiss this time. His mouth moved gently against hers in a series of soft, nibbling little kisses that threatened to drain the marrow from her bones.

"You're beautiful," he whispered, burying his face in her hair. "You're the most beautiful woman I've ever seen."

"Don't." Devon said, but her voice was faint and papery, and when Ryan nuzzled the hair away form her neck and slowly began kissing his way down its length, she moaned.

"Put your arms around me," he whispered.

No, she thought, no, don't do it.

But her hands were already slipping up his chest, linking behind his neck; her fingers were digging into the silky dark hair that touched his collar.

"We can't," she said in a choked voice. "Ryan, please..."

Ryan kissed her, his mouth soft and cool on hers. Her lips parted, but only a little; she began to tremble in his arms.

His body was hardening like steel. She wanted him, he knew it, but she was holding back. It was almost as if she were new to this, as if the sensations his mouth and hands were arousing in her were sensations she had never felt before.

It was a parody of innocence. He knew that. But knowing it didn't lessen its impact. His breathing quickened as he drew her closer against him. Her heart was racing; he could feel it leap against his. He swept his hand over her body, down the long, clean line of her spine to her rounded bottom, then up again to cup her breast.

Her response was swift and electric. She made a soft, keening sound of surrender and thrust herself against him, her pelvis pressed against his, her breast hardening to fill his palm.

He had to have her. Now, here, on the desk or on the couch or on the damned floor, it didn't matter which. All he knew was his overwhelming need.

With a groan, he swept the tweed jacket from her shoulders.

"Devon," he said thickly.

The door flew open.

"Mr. Kincaid!"

Devon sprang back at the sound of Sylvia's voice. Her gaze flew to the secretary's face. The woman looked shocked. No. Not just shocked. Amused. Delighted.

Why wouldn't she be? Devon spun toward the window. It wasn't every day a secretary walked into her boss's office and found him in the middle of a seduction—though for all she knew, seductions were the norm around here. With a man like Ryan Kincaid, anything was possible.

But not with her. All her life she'd been called "cold." Bettina said she had a cold heart; the girls at school said she was a cold fish. And the few men she'd dated had used a word that was much crueler.

And yet the touch of a man she knew just well enough to hate had sent her flying out of control. If his secretary hadn't come in just then...

"Dammit, Sylvia," Ryan said gruffly, "this had better be good."

"Oh, Mr. Kincaid, I'm terribly sorry, sir."

She didn't sound sorry at all, Ryan thought grimly. She sounded like a woman who was doing what she could to keep from bursting into laughter, but then, he could hardly blame her. He hadn't been found in such a compromising situation since he was eighteen and he and half a dozen fraternity brothers had been caught making a raid on the women's dorm at college.

"I tried the intercom, sir, but you must have shut off the phone. And I knocked. But, uh, you must have been preoccupied with your, ah, your niece. And—"

She looked at Devon. Ryan did, too. She was staring out the window. Her face, seen in profile, was white and pinched with embarrassment.

He thought of how flushed that same face had been moments ago. She'd been so filled with passion that he'd almost taken her right here in his office. Hell, he *would* have taken her, if Sylvia hadn't...

Ryan took a deep breath and thrust his hand through his hair.

"And?"

"Your grandfather is on the line. He said it was important, so—"

Ryan waved his hand in dismissal, sat down at his desk, and reached for the telephone.

"Grandfather?"

Great, Devon thought, just great. It wasn't enough she'd had to endure the gathering of the Kincaids Friday evening; was she now expected to sit through another clan meeting?

Forget it, she thought. She walked to Ryan's desk, reached out and slapped her palm over the telephone mouthpiece. Ryan looked up, frowning.

"Just be sure you remember to call the old boy off," Devon snapped.

Ryan reached out a proprietary hand and wrapped it around her wrist. She glared back at him.

"If you try anything, I'll scream so loud they'll hear me in New Jersey."

His eyes narrowed to green slits. "Hang on a moment, will you?" he said into the phone. Then he muffled it against his chest and glared back at her. "Just where do you think you're going?"

"Anyplace you're not."

"I'm talking to my grandfather."

"How fortunate for you both. Be sure to tell him that I can't marry you because I'm already engaged to a Martian."

"I hope you'll both be very happy." His hand tightened on hers. "Just stay tuned."

Ryan took a breath, exhaled it, then put the phone to his ear again.

"Grandfather," he said, "I'm glad you called. Devon is here."

"Oh. How nice."

"Actually, she's upset. She, ah, she just found out that—I know it's an error, of course—"

"That's exactly what I called to tell you, my boy. I made an error. About Devon."

Ryan could feel the weight lifting from his shoulders. He let go of Devon, looked at her, and made an okay sign with his thumb and forefinger.

"I'm happy to hear you admit it, sir."

"I was so concerned that Bettina would find a way to get her hands on any money I might settle on the girl that I ignored the obvious. A fund can be established so that only a specified amount **per** month can be withdrawn."

Ryan smiled. "Of course."

"It will give the girl a feeling of independence. Anyway, now that I've had a better look at her, I'm fairly certain she can fend for herself."

Ryan's lips drew back from his teeth. "She's not exactly the compliant little thing you thought she was, is she?"

"As I said the other night, Ryan, a little spirit never hurt. Keeps things interesting."

"I'm really glad you've thought this through, sir. I know you meant well, but—"

"But I hadn't taken all the details into account. Yes, I know. Well, now I have and I think it's a much improved solution, don't you?"

"Definitely."

"Would you be willing to work out the details of the trust with me and my attorney?"

For the first time in days, Ryan began to breathe easy. Freedom, he thought, freedom.

"Of course, sir."

"Believe me, Ryan. This is for the best. I know I'm pressuring you—"

Ryan smiled. "Grandfather, you have my solemn word. I'm more than happy to do this for you."

The old man gave a contented sigh. "In that case, I should like everything settled as soon as possible."

"Yes. So would I." The sooner Devon Franklin was out of his life, the better.

"That's the spirit."

"Well, you know me, sir. Once I say I'll do something, I don't like putting it off."

"Shall we agree on a day this week, then?"

Ryan looked at Devon. She was watching him with the wariness most people reserved for rattlesnakes but he didn't care. She could loathe him as much as she liked, now that she was almost out of his life.

He opened his appointment book and thumbed through it. How long could it take to meet with James's lawyer and discuss setting up a trust fund? An hour? Two?

"I'm free Friday afternoon," he said after a minute. "How does four o'clock sound?"

"It sounds perfect." James gave another deep sigh. "I must say, my boy, you've been very understanding."

Ryan smiled and tilted back his chair. "Anything to make you happy, sir. You know that."

"I know you may not see it clearly now, but I'm certain that someday you'll realize the great benefits to this marriage."

Ryan's stomach, and his chair, fell forward with a bang.

"What?"

"The trust will keep Devon from feeling as if she's at your mercy. Oh, you'll be happy to know, I've spoken with Bettina. She's thrilled with the news." James chuckled. "Especially since I told her

I'm deeding Gordon's house over to her as a sort of reverse dowry."

Ryan's body jerked as if an electric current had passed through it.

"Hold it," he said. "Just hold it right there! I never agreed to—"

"What's the matter?" Devon interjected.

He looked up at her. "Just take it easy—"

"I am taking it easy, my boy. In fact, I feel more relaxed than I have in weeks."

"Not you, Grandfather. I was talking to..." He jammed his fingers through his hair so that the dark strands curled down over his forehead. "Listen here, Grandfather, I never meant—"

"Friday's an excellent day for the wedding. In fact," James said slyly, "I'd already thought of that day myself. And I've given some thought to the plans."

"Dammit, sir—"

"I know, I know. Brimley said I was behaving like a tyrant, but honestly, Ryan, can you think of a better place for the ceremony than the library right here in this house? Brimley can make herself useful, handling details. Champagne, petits fours, flowers—"

Ryan shot to his feet. "Wait a minute! I wasn't talking about—"

"—any fuss. I understand, but a glass or two of Mumm's isn't fussing, is it? I've already spoken with Judge Wiggins. You remember him, don't you? He says he'll be delighted to perform the ceremony."

"Great Caesar's ghost," Ryan whispered, "you've thought of everything!"

"I was going to call an announcement in to the *Times* but that secretary of yours—what is her name?—was kind enough to offer to do it for me."

"Sylvia?" Ryan said numbly. "Sylvia knows?"

"She didn't want to interrupt you, my boy. I had to tell her why this call was so urgent, didn't I?"

Ryan grasped at the telephone cord like a drowning man grabbing at a lifeline.

"Grandfather," he said, "I hate to spoil this for you, but—"

"There is one last thing, Ryan. I saw my doctor this morning."

Ryan froze. The old man's voice had softened in a way that suggested what came next would be something of a shock.

"And? What did he say?"

James fairly cackled with glee. "He said it was a miracle, that I look like a man with a new lease on life. The charlatan is taking credit for it, of course, but I know the truth. It's your agreeing to this marriage that's made all the difference."

Ryan's mouth opened, then shut. He groaned softly and closed his eyes.

"Let's see . . . Have I left anything out?"

"Nothing," Ryan said miserably, "not a damned thing."

"Excellent. I'll see you Friday." James cleared his throat. "Ryan? Thank you, son. You've made an old man's last days very, very happy."

The phone went dead.

For a second or two, Ryan sat frozen at his desk. Then he yanked the phone from his ear and stared in horror at an instrument that seemed to have suddenly metamorphosed into a tarantula.

"Hell," he snarled. "Bloody hell!"

"What's wrong?" Devon said. "You look as if you've seen a ghost. And I didn't hear you say one word to your grandfather about this insane plotting and scheming of his." Ryan didn't answer and she leaned over the desk and jabbed her finger at him. "Call him back. Tell him not to contact my mother again. Tell him—"

She jumped sky-high as Ryan gave a roar of rage. Leaping to his feet, he pulled the phone from the wall, tossed it on the floor, and pointed an accusing finger right back at Devon.

"Which one of you put this idea in his head?" he snarled. "You? Or your mother?"

"What idea?" Devon tried not to shrink back as he stalked around the desk and towered over her. "What are you talking about?"

"I hope you're proud of yourself, lady. I hope you're damned proud! It's not every day a mother-daughter act as bad as yours has a chance of succeeding!"

"Are you going to tell me what's going on?"

Ryan took a deep breath. "I'll tell you what's going on." A smile was curling across his mouth, one so coldly feral that Devon felt her heart stop beating. "Give the ring back to your Martian boyfriend," he said. "Friday afternoon, you're going to become my blushing bride."

CHAPTER FIVE

DEVON tried to speak but at first she couldn't manage anything more than a strangled croak.

Finally she licked her lips, swallowed hard, and choked out a sentence.

"Wha—what did you say?"

The terrible smile vanished from Ryan's face. He jammed his hands into his trouser pockets, walked to the window, and stared out into the street.

"I said, there's no way out of it. The marriage is on."

The marriage is on? His marriage, to her? Her marriage, to him? Was he crazy?

"The ceremony's Friday at four o'clock."

Ryan's voice was hard and clipped, his tone almost matter-of-fact. There was no longer any question about it. He *was* crazy!

Devon marched to where Ryan stood and tapped him on the shoulder. When he turned, she jammed her hands onto her hips and glared at him.

"I don't want to ruin this for you," she snapped, "but you've left out one minor detail." Her chin lifted and she pounded her fist into her chest. "Me! Me, dammit! Marriage takes two, or had you forgotten? I am one of the principal parties in this lunatic scheme, or had you overlooked that?"

"How could I possibly overlook it? It's not every day a man has his bride handpicked for him."

"Stop calling me that," Devon said fiercely. "I am *not* your bride!"

"Not yet, you aren't. But you will be, come Friday afternoon."

She watched him, waited for him to laugh in derision or explode in fury. She waited for him to curse, march to the phone, call his fruitcake of a grandfather and tell him what he could do with his off-the-wall matchmaking.

But Ryan didn't do anything. He just stood there, his face looking as if it were made of granite, and it was that stony acceptance that finally made her start to tremble.

"I don't know what's going on here," she said unsteadily, "but if you think I'd ever really go along with this..."

"The idea of marrying you thrills me as much as it thrills you."

"Then call your grandfather! Ryan, the longer you let this go on—"

"It's too late."

"What do you mean, it's too late! Get on that phone, dammit! Tell that insane old man that there can't be a wedding without a bride."

"There's a bride," Ryan said grimly. "A sweet, apple-cheeked, demure, old-fashioned slip of a girl with a hard right, a tough mouth, and a disposition that would make a rhino blush."

"Get this into your head, Ryan Kincaid. I will not marry you."

"You have no choice."

"What do you mean, I have no choice?" Devon stamped her foot. "In case you hadn't noticed, this is not the Middle Ages! Kings don't tell their subjects who to marry, and when.''

"Devon, calm down and listen.''

"No. No, *you* listen! Maybe you're in the habit of letting Grandpa tell you not just when to jump but how high, but—''

"I've never let him tell me anything,'' Ryan said wearily.

"But you're going to let him tell you when—and whom—to marry?''

Ryan took a deep breath. "I don't expect you to understand.''

"Try me.''

He hesitated. "My grandfather is dying.''

"Oh.'' Devon chewed on her lower lip. "That's...that's too bad.'' Her brows drew together. "But making human sacrifices out of us isn't going to change that, now is it?''

Ryan sighed and turned toward her. "Sit down, Devon,'' he said quietly. "We've got a lot to discuss.''

"If I were you, the only person I'd discuss anything with is a good shrink. And I'd climb onto his couch as soon as I could manage it.''

She started toward the door, her walk brisk, but she hadn't gotten very far before Ryan reached out and clapped a hand on her shoulder.

"Sit down, Devon.''

"What for?''

"I told you, we have things to talk about.''

Devon shook free of his hand. "We have nothing to talk about,'' she said coldly.

"My grandfather's going to set up a trust fund in your name.''

"Thrilling news. Unfortunately, I don't want a trust fund. I don't want anything but to go back to California and forget I ever laid eyes on you or him."

"I've decided to match it with a second lump sum payment, one that comes due after an appropriate length of time."

"Even more thrilling. Dammit, Ryan—"

"That's the good news," Ryan said smoothly, as if she hadn't spoken. "The bad news is that you also get a wedding ring."

"I don't *want* a wedding ring. I don't want you. And I won't have you. The very thought of marrying you is... is— "

"Believe me, there's nothing you can say about the idea that I wouldn't agree with."

"You're wasting your breath, telling that to me. Tell it to your grandfather."

"I did." Ryan shrugged his shoulders. "He disagrees."

"Dammit all, how can you stand there and say that so calmly?"

"What I really want to do," Ryan said with icy precision, "is punch my fist straight through the wall. It sure as hell might make me feel better—but it wouldn't change a damned thing." His hands closed on her shoulders and he shoved her, none too gently, into a chair. "Now take a couple of deep breaths so you can think straight, and maybe between us, we can come up with something to get us out of this mess."

Devon watched as he began pacing back and forth. She could see that he wasn't anywhere near as calm as she'd thought. Well, that was something. At least she wasn't standing out on the edge of this cliff alone.

"Is your grandfather senile?" she asked.

Ryan laughed. "He's about as senile as a fox."

She nodded. "Is he bored, then? Maybe if you... if you could arrange for him to do something to occupy his time—"

"He is not senile. He is not bored. He's just decided to meddle in my life, dammit." Ryan paused, his back to her. She saw his shoulders rise and fall as he took several deep breaths. "I have to keep telling myself that he means well."

"He means well?" Devon echoed hysterically and shot to her feet. "What good does that do me? He means well, indeed! So did the guy who tied Joan of Arc to the stake!" She took a deep breath and turned toward the door. "Goodbye, Ryan. You're in a fix, but it's got nothing to do with me."

Ryan got to the door just as she did. He slapped his hands on either side of her, imprisoning her between his arms.

Trapped, she swung around to face him.

"Get away from me or I'll scream."

He laughed softly. "You'd be wasting your time, baby. After the little scene Sylvia walked in on a few minutes ago, she'd take the sound of you screaming as a vote of feminine satisfaction."

Color flew into Devon's cheeks. "What a bastard you are!"

"Let's stick to the subject, if you don't mind."

"There is no subject. Not that involves me, at any rate."

His smile was quick and chill. "No?"

"No."

"Is that what you're going to tell Mama?"

It was a shot that hit home. Devon fought to keep her expression from giving anything away.

"I don't know what you mean."

"Come on, Devon. Don't play dumb. It doesn't suit you. James decided you and I would make a perfect pair. He told that to your mother. And I've told you I see no way out of the situation. Now, what do you think Bettina's going to do when you tell her that you said 'no'?"

Devon swallowed, and Ryan smiled coldly.

"Cat got your tongue? When you tell her you turned your back on this once-in-a-lifetime offer, she'll explode with a bang that'll make Krakatoa sound like a firecracker. To put it succinctly, she'll go bananas."

Devon stared up at him, her eyes huge and dark.

"She'll call you every kind of fool, and she'll keep at it day and night."

Bettina would do more than that, Devon knew. She would sob out stories of a life of struggle and sacrifice. She'd accuse Devon of turning her back on her the way her father had.

"And she'll never let you forget that the house she and my brother lived in in San Francisco would have been deeded over to her, if you'd married me."

"No," Devon whispered, "you can't—"

"She'll never let you rest or forget what you've denied her. And, sooner or later, just to get her off your back, you'll give up the fight and agree to become Mrs. Ryan Kincaid."

Devon's mouth trembled. "All right," she whispered. "Suppose, just for the sake of argument, my mother did want me to... want me to..." She swallowed hard. "I suppose...I suppose I can think of reasons why she might...might encourage me to...to accept your grandfather's offer. But...but why would your grandfather do this? I know what he thinks of my mother. Why would he want me— her daughter—to marry you?" She tried to smile. "Maybe he's read Pygmalion one time too many."

"It's that school of yours. He thinks it taught you to be a good wife."

"It taught me everything I'd need to know if they decided to turn the clock back a couple of hundred years," she said bitterly.

"He finds that part of your charm." Ryan's mouth twisted. "He thinks the perfect wife is one who's never noticed that the twentieth century's almost over."

"Well, tell that old reprobate he made a mistake. He wanted a woman who was brainless, opinionless, and compliant." Devon's head lifted in defiance. "I am none of those things."

She was other things, though, Ryan thought as he looked down at her. She was sexy and beautiful, and whether it was one hell of an act or some unbelievable truth, there was an innocence to her that made him want—that made him want...

He frowned, dropped his hands to his sides, and stepped back.

"I've told him that," he said bluntly.

"And?"

Ryan sighed as he made his way across the room. Frank might laugh and say thirty-two wasn't middle-aged, but hell, right now he felt older than Methuselah.

"And," Ryan said gloomily, sinking slowly into the chair behind his desk, "he said that was OK, that he liked your spirit."

Devon stared at him. It was easier now, marshaling her thoughts without Ryan leaning over her, standing so close that she could see the faint stubble on his firm chin, the thin black lines that rimmed his green irises.

"Let me get this straight," she said slowly. "Your grandfather decided that the daughter of a woman he despises will make you a good wife because she can embroider Bless This House on a tea towel and trade insults with you at the same time?"

"I know it sounds strange—"

"It sounds demented."

"Look, there are other factors."

"Name one."

"My brother, Gordon. He said he wanted to provide for your welfare—"

Devon forced back the almost overwhelming desire to break into hysterical laughter.

"Don't you think trying to marry me off to you is taking the concept of 'welfare' just a little too far?"

"Yes," Ryan snapped, "I sure as hell do!"

"So?"

"So," he snarled, jumping to his feet, "I'm stuck with this stupid promise I made the old man, to carry out whatever last wish he asked of me."

She couldn't help it. This time, a strangled bark of laughter burst from her throat. Ryan glowered at her, his eyes blazing.

"You think this is funny?" he growled.

"No. No! It isn't funny at all. It's...it's incredible. It's like a play written by a madman and directed by an idiot."

"It's not a play," Ryan said grimly. "It's real life. My life, dammit. And unless we work something out, we're going to find ourselves cornered into riding off on a honeymoon Friday afternoon."

Devon's giddy smile faded. She felt behind her for a chair and sat down carefully, her eyes on Ryan's.

"You're right."

"Of course I'm right."

"What can we do about it?"

It was, Ryan thought, one hell of a terrific question. He sighed, flexed his shoulders, and sat down across from her.

"Let me think."

The minutes ticked away while he sat there, his head in his hands. Then, slowly, he looked up and began to smile.

"What?" Devon said breathlessly.

"I think I've got an answer. Did you ever hear of a leasing agreement?"

The hope that had begun to shine in Devon's eyes faded.

"A what?" she whispered.

"A leasing agreement." Ryan yanked open the bottom drawer of his desk, flipped through the files, yanked out a sheaf of papers and dropped them on the blotter. "Here," he said, "take a look at this."

Devon rose slowly and came around to his side of the desk. Ryan watched her as she bent over the papers and began scanning them. Her hair spilled forward over her shoulders like skeins of silk.

Ryan's nostrils flared. No L'Air du Temps today. She smelled instead of something more subtle. Lilies of the valley, maybe, or roses. Whatever it was, the scent was soft and delightfully feminine.

His gaze went to her hand. She'd placed it on the desk to anchor the papers. It was such a small hand. The fingers, though, were long and slender; there was a tiny red line across one knuckle, a paper cut, it looked like, and with dizzying swiftness, Ryan was almost overwhelmed by the desire to take her hand in his, lift it to his lips, and soothe the tiny, angry cut with his tongue.

He pulled back, his frown deepening, and snatched up the papers.

"Here," he said irritably, "all you have to really read is this last page."

She read it. Then she looked at him, her eyes puzzled.

"According to this, you own a Porsche."

"Dammit, I do not *own* the Porsche. That's the whole point." Ryan stabbed his finger at the document. "I *lease* it," he said. "At the end of a year, the car goes back to the dealer. I never have to see it again, it never has to see me."

Devon gave a little laugh. "I must be missing something here."

Ryan sighed. He stood, drew the chair from the other side of his desk to where she stood, and motioned her into it.

"Let me try sketching out the details," he said. He pulled a yellow legal pad and a pen toward him. "My attorney—and yours, if you wish—can flesh it out later, but maybe I can give you the general idea."

Devon watched as he bent over the yellow pad, scrawling words across it in a wide, loose hand. Her mouth narrowed as she watched him. What an absolutely impossible human being he was. So smug. So self-confident. So damnably good-looking and sexy.

What would have happened before, if his secretary hadn't come bursting in? Would she really have let Ryan make love to her?

It was crazy but she could still feel the heat of his body, the hardness of his arousal. She could still taste his kiss on her lips...

She jumped as he tossed down his pen.

"That'll do it," he said.

Devon licked her lips nervously. "That'll do what?"

He smiled and pushed the yellow pad toward her.

"Take a look and you'll see," he said, but she couldn't see anything. She couldn't concentrate on anything, except Ryan's closeness.

He had risen from his chair and now he was bending over her, his hands resting on the desk on either side of her, his cheek almost pressed against her hair.

Her breathing quickened. All she had to do was tilt her head back, turn her face just an inch toward his. His mouth would be a whisper from hers...

"Well?" he said, "what do you think?"

A little shudder went through her and she drew away from him, until her spine was tightly pressed against the back of the chair.

"I—I'm not very good at reading legalese, Ryan. Why don't you explain it to me?"

"It's only pseudo-legalese," he said with a little laugh. "It'll take a couple of attorneys to change this into truly indecipherable jargon."

Devon breathed a quick sigh of relief as he picked up the pad, turned and leaned back against the desk. It was easier to think without him close to her. She still couldn't make sense of what he was saying, except to know that it was about trust funds and lump-sum settlements and deeds and tax payments.

"Tax payments?" she said, interrupting him.

Ryan looked up, his eyes cool. "All right, I'll push it to three years. But not a day more than that. Bettina will have to find a way to maintain the place on her own by then."

Devon stared at him. "I don't know what you're talking about."

"Dammit," he said angrily, "haven't you heard a word I said?" He tossed the legal pad on the desk and bent over her again. "I'm talking about a contract," he said, slapping his hand against the pad. "One that leaves nothing to chance."

"What kind of contract? And how would it prevent our... our—marriage from taking place?"

"It wouldn't. But it would define its terms so there'd be no surprises. All the arrangements of your settlement would be spelled out—"

"Are we back to that? I told you—"

"—and the transfer of the deed of Gordon's house to Bettina—"

"Dammit," Devon said, jumping to her feet, "you've missed the point. I am not—"

"And we will both agree," Ryan said calmly, "that we will review our situation at the end of a six-month trial period."

"Don't be ridiculous! I would never..." Devon's eyebrows lifted. "What do you mean, a six-month trial period?"

"I mean just that," he answered. "Six months from Friday, my bank will automatically transfer the monetary settlement we agree upon into your private account. And then we'll sit down and decide if there's any reason to sign on for another half year."

"You mean, if James is still... if he's still..."

"Alive," Ryan said bluntly. "Yes, that's exactly what I mean."

"Surely, he wouldn't agree..."

"He doesn't have to. I want him to be happy, Devon, but there's no way I'm going to lock myself into a nightmare for the rest of my life." He smiled tightly. "Well? What do you think?"

"I think you're as crazy as your grandfather! First you make it sound as if there's some gilt-edged morality in keeping an impossible promise to him. Then you turn around and come up with a way to turn the promise into a farce."

"It's a perfectly logical escape clause." Ryan's lips twitched in a cool smile. "What's the matter, baby? Did you really think I'd let this go on forever?"

"Only fools believe in forever, Ryan. And whatever you think I am, I promise you, I am not a fool."

"No. No, I don't think you are. Which is why I'm so certain you'll see the benefits to our marriage. Everybody comes out a winner. Bettina gets her house, James gets what he wants, and neither you nor I have to feel that we're signing our lives away."

Devon looked down at the legal pad again. What he'd outlined was all so reasonable—assuming you could agree in the first place that it was reasonable for two people who despised each other to marry at all.

Not that what he'd described would actually be a marriage. It would be a contract. A...a leasing arrangement, subject to renewal after six months.

She cleared her throat. "There's nothing in this about—about sex," she said.

His expression didn't change. "No. There isn't."

Why did it suddenly seem too difficult to draw breath?

"Well, there should be. I mean, if I were to agree—if you and I went through with this..."

"The deed to the house, the trust fund, the final monetary settlement I'll make on you...all of that can be written into a contract." Lazy laughter suddenly glinted in Ryan's eyes. "But I'll be damned if I can think of a way to define the terms of a man and woman's sexual relationship in a legal document."

"You mean, their lack of a sexual relationship," Devon said, forcing her gaze not to waver from his. "I wouldn't sleep with you, Ryan. You'd have to understand that."

An insolent smile curled across his mouth. "Wouldn't you?"

He moved toward her with the grace of a jungle cat. Devon felt her blood drumming in her veins.

But you never ran from a predatory beast; you stood your ground and faced it, no matter what it took in courage.

She waited until he was a breath away before tilting her head up and meeting his smile with her own.

"Poor Ryan," she said softly. "Is that what this is all about? Do you need Grandpa to get you a bed playmate?" Her smile vanished. "Because if it is, you're out of luck. I'd sooner sleep with a snake."

She thought, at first, he was going to strike her. She could see the sharp, swift blaze of anger that turned his eyes a green so dark it was almost black. Then, at what seemed the last instant, a muscle in his jaw twitched. A smile worked its way across his lips again; he reached out and ran the tip of one finger over her slightly parted lips.

"If it makes you feel safer to think that, then go right on fooling yourself."

"Don't do that," she said sharply, twisting away from the tormenting stroke of his finger.

Ryan laughed softly. "I wouldn't have to coerce you into my bed, Devon. We both know that."

"You mean, you *couldn't* coerce me into it."

He shrugged. "Phrase it any way you like, lover. The bottom line is the same. I've never had to force a woman into my bed. And I'm sure as hell not about to start with you."

"Good. Because there's no other way you'd get me there."

His arms slipped around her. She didn't struggle, nor did she yield as he drew her closely against him.

"Is that a challenge, Devon?"

Was it? Devon's heart began to race. She thought of how he'd kissed her a little while ago, of how it had felt to have his hands on her and his tongue in her mouth.

"No," she said, just a little breathlessly. "It's not a challenge, it's a certainty."

Ryan smiled. "In that case," he said softly, "you might as well agree to this marriage. What have you got to lose?"

She didn't answer but he could read her thoughts in the darkness of those huge violet eyes. He knew she was thinking that there was really no way out of this and suddenly he wondered what her eyes would look like if they were shining with happiness, if he were a man she loved and wanted, a man whose kisses she longed for.

His arms fell away from her. He turned, walked to his desk, and sat down.

"Well?" he said brusquely. "What's it going to be, Devon? Are we on for Friday or aren't we?"

He sounded as if he were talking about a golf date, she thought, and then she took a deep, deep breath and did the only logical thing.

She said yes.

CHAPTER SIX

IT WAS, as a wise man once said, déjà vu all over again.

Ryan was standing at the head of a flower-bedecked aisle with Frank just behind him. Music was playing softly in the background and a smiling justice of the peace was waiting patiently for events to begin.

"Frank?" Ryan whispered out of the side of his mouth. "Frank, what am I doing here?"

Frank lifted his second Scotch and soda to his lips. "A good question," he said, "to which I have an even better answer. It's your life, pal. Why ask me?"

Right, Ryan thought. It *was* his life. And, just about now, it was time for him to wake up and find out that this was all a bad dream.

Except it wasn't. It was all frighteningly real. He was about to be married, to a woman he didn't know, didn't trust, didn't like...

"Ryan?"

Ryan blinked. Agnes Brimley, decked out in a flowered dress and tiny veiled hat, had sidled up beside him.

"Would you like me to go and see what's keeping your lovely bride, dear?"

"Dear" was a word new to Miss Brimley's vocabulary but everything about her today was new. Different, anyway. She was fairly bubbling with excitement, but then, she seemed to be the only person in the room who didn't know this whole damned wedding was a farce.

The old witch had smiled more today than in all the years Ryan had known her.

He thought of how quickly that smile would vanish if she went searching for Devon and found her curled somewhere in a corner, refusing to let Bettina drag her out, and he sighed.

"Thanks," he said, and forced a smile to his lips. "I'll go and get her myself."

"Are you sure, Ryan, dear?" Brimley's lips twitched. "Some say it's bad luck for the groom to see the bride before the ceremony."

Ryan's mouth thinned. "There's no danger of that for Devon and me, Miss Brimley," he said.

Ignoring Frank's faint, indelicate snort of laughter, Ryan went in search of his future wife.

Bettina snapped the top on her lipstick, popped it into her purse, and frowned at Devon, who was standing stiffly on the opposite side of the enormous first floor powder room.

"I just wish you'd bought something new to wear, darling. You don't look terribly festive."

Devon turned slowly and looked into the mirror.

No. She certainly didn't look festive. Ryan's secretary had telephoned two days ago to tell her that Ryan had opened accounts for her at Saks and Henri Bendel and Galleries Lafayette; she had *carte blanche* to buy whatever she wanted. And for her mother, too, if she wished.

Bettina had given a whoop at the news but her exhilaration had changed to disbelief and then irritation when Devon had refused to go off on a shopping spree.

"You're marrying a very wealthy—and, I might add, very generous—husband," her mother had said crossly. "The least you can do is show him the courtesy of accepting his generosity."

Devon hadn't bothered commenting on the flawed logic, she'd simply said she had her own clothing and jewelry and didn't need anything from Ryan.

"Surely, you can at least buy a wedding dress," Bettina had insisted.

Devon had suddenly thought of how thrilling it would be to choose a gown if she were marrying Ryan because he truly loved her, a gown that would make his incredible green eyes light with admiration, a gown he would later strip slowly from her body while the look in his eyes went from reverence to passion.

She'd wondered how it would be to let him finish undressing her; how it would feel to have his hands caress her breasts. She'd imagined the heat that would flare between her thighs, the fevered moment when he slipped his hands beneath her hips, lifted her to him and joined his body to hers...

For no reason at all, her eyes had filled with tears.

"I'm not buying a wedding dress," she'd said fiercely, swiping at her eyes with the back of her hand, and Bettina had flounced out of the hotel to shop on her own.

Now, Bettina was dressed to the teeth in a hot pink silk suit with a matching hat and snakeskin pumps. New bracelets jingled on one wrist; a jeweled watch winked on the other. Heavy gold earrings glinted at her ears and clouds of Chanel No. 5 wafted into the air as she waited impatiently for her daughter.

Devon gazed into the mirror. She was mouselike by comparison. Except for the almost feverish glow in her cheeks, her face was deathly white; her eyes, and the shadows beneath them, looked funereal. Her hair was drawn back and secured with a gold clip at the nape of her neck. She wore a simple blue dress with no accessories.

Devon's mouth trembled. No, she didn't look festive, but why should she? There was nothing "festive" about realizing you'd agreed to sell yourself into a sham of a marriage.

What a fool she'd been, letting Ryan badger her into agreeing to this! How could she have let it happen? She'd known it was a mistake within minutes of having said she'd become his wife and she'd tried to tell him so, but by then it had been too late.

He had already made phone calls—to his attorney, to James's attorney, to James himself, and finally to Bettina.

"It's done," he'd said, his face cold, and Devon had thought suddenly of how a fly must feel as the final bit of the spider's silk wraps tightly around it.

Then he'd smiled politely and said he hoped she understood but he had tons of work to do. A beaming Sylvia had whisked her into the elevator, out the front door, and into a taxi. And when the cab reached the hotel, Bettina had come racing out, dizzy with excitement.

There'd been no further calls from Ryan, no visits. Nothing. The only reminder of the terrible bargain she'd made had been Sylvia's phone call informing her that she was free to spend his money, now that she'd agreed to become his wife.

A chill swept along Devon's spine. She could feel it penetrate the marrow of her bones.

"I can't," she whispered to her reflection. "Oh, I can't!"

"Did you say something, darling?"

She swung toward Bettina, who was sitting on the edge of a chair, carefully smoothing her stockings.

"I said that I can't go through with this."

"Don't be ridiculous, Devon."

"I must have been out of my mind, agreeing to marry Ryan Kincaid!"

"It's just bridal jitters. I remember when I married the first time—"

"Bridal jitters? Mother, what are you talking about? I'm not a bride, I'm a...a puppet, with you and the Kincaids pulling the strings."

"Stop that! You're talking nonsense."

"I don't even know this man," Devon said, her voice rising. "And what little I do know, I don't like."

"Nonsense. Ryan is handsome, he's wealthy—what more do you need to know?"

"Marriage is supposed to be about love, not—not promises and contracts."

"Marriage is always about promises and contracts," Bettina said coldly. "The only difference in this arrangement is that everything's out in the open. Ryan's told you what he expects of you and

what you may expect of him. You should be grateful
for his honesty.''

"It's not honesty, it's manipulation!'' Devon
flung out her arms. "How did I get myself into this
mess?''

"Devon! Devon, you listen to me—''

"No. I'm not listening to anybody but myself
this time.''

"Will you stop being such a fool? Who could
have dreamed we'd come away with all this? A bit
of cash, perhaps. That was the best we could have
hoped for. Now we've got the house, a trust fund,
a marriage that could last long enough to be prof-
itable, if you play your cards right, and suddenly
you're panicking.''

"No,'' Devon cried, "no—''

"Listen to Mama, Devon.'' Devon spun around.
Ryan stood just inside the doorway, his face looking
as if it had been chiseled in granite. "You know
she's right. This is no time to turn tail and run, not
with the brass ring just within your reach.''

Devon wanted to tell him that he was wrong, that
she'd anticipated nothing from him or from James,
but the denial stuck in her throat. He would never
believe her; she would only end up sounding as if
she were groveling and she'd sooner ride to hell on
horseback than do that.

As if on cue, the soft sounds of "Oh, Promise
Me'' drifted softly into the room. Ryan smiled
coolly.

"We're on,'' he said, and held out his arm.

"Go on.'' Bettina practically hissed the words.
"Just do it and get it over with.''

And with those tender words ringing in her ears, Devon put her hand on Ryan's arm and let him lead her down the steps to become his wife.

It was not the sort of ceremony that made for fond memories.

Bettina, her mouth drawn into a determined line, positioned herself just behind Devon as if to block her exit should she suddenly decide to bolt and run.

Frank, still looking shell-shocked at the news that had been dropped on him two days before, positioned himself close beside Ryan.

"To help you get out the door," he muttered, "when you come to your senses."

Agnes Brimley broke into sobs midway through the ceremony, surprising everyone, especially the judge, who'd started things off with a pleasant homily about man and woman and the joys of wedlock before looking into the faces of the couple standing before him. Then he'd cleared his throat and delivered the brief words of the civil code that ended with Ryan and Devon being pronounced man and wife.

"You may kiss the bride," the judge said.

Ryan turned to Devon. The look on her face was unbelievable. Her lips were curled with disdain; her eyes flashed a message that only a fool would misunderstand. Hands off, it read; you're not permitted to touch me.

It was the way she'd looked at him the day they'd met in Montano's. But Ryan knew better now. Whatever she thought of him or he thought of her, he could drive that icy look from her pale, beautiful face in a heartbeat. All he had to do was take her in his arms, part her lips with his and she would make that little sound of surrender that drove him crazy. Her hands would lift and link behind his neck; her eyes would glaze with desire.

He could have her whenever he wanted her, and she knew it.

"You have to kiss your bride," James said with a soft chuckle, "so that I can kiss her, too."

Ryan gritted his teeth and put his arms around Devon. He drew her toward him, feeling the tension in her body. The look in her eyes changed, going from icy contempt to dark apprehension. Her mouth—that soft, rose-petal mouth—uncurled and began to tremble and all at once, he remembered what she'd said about this not being the Middle Ages, when marriages were arranged.

Was this how a bride would have looked at her groom all those centuries ago, with the terrifying fear of the unknown in her eyes? A woman would have known that the end of the marriage ceremony was only the beginning, that she had yet to face the night and the moment when her lord and master came to her in their bridal chamber and locked the door behind him.

"Dammit," Frank muttered, "kiss the babe and get it over with, OK?"

Ryan's heartbeat rocketed. He clasped Devon's face between his hands. Slowly, his eyes locked with hers, he bent to her and kissed her gently, his lips barely parting hers.

He felt the sudden tremor sweep through her, a tremor he knew she'd tried, and failed, to prevent. Fire licked along his veins and his arms went around her, his mouth never leaving hers. His kiss deepened, his lips moving over hers, the tip of his tongue making a hidden, silken foray into her mouth. The faintest sound rose in her throat, trembled on her lips as it passed from her kiss to his mouth.

Pop!

The cork exploded from a bottle of champagne under the expert touch of the caterer Miss Brimley had hired.

Ryan stared down into Devon's flushed face. "Devon..." he said softly.

"Congratulations, young man," the judge said.

"Good luck, my boy," James said. "I know you've done the right thing."

Frank was more direct. "Old pal," he said glumly, "I think you've lost your marbles."

Ryan looked at his bride again. She was standing as far from him as she could get and still be in the same room. Miss Brimley was on one side of her, Bettina on the other. They were both babbling away and Devon was nodding her head as if she were listening, but Ryan knew instinctively that she wasn't. As he watched, the pink tip of her tongue snaked out and lightly touched the center of her bottom lip where an almost indiscernible swelling remained as the passionate mark of his kiss.

His body knotted like a fist. Hell, he thought, and suddenly he wondered if Frank might not be right.

At dusk, Ryan stabbed his key into the lock of the ornate oak door of his three-story brownstone in the East Sixties. Devon stood beside him, her shoulder brushing his.

Married, he thought. I am married.

He knew it intellectually. But that didn't change the fact that he sure as hell didn't feel married. It had all happened so quickly—he'd been a bachelor on Monday and now here it was, only Friday, and he was a husband.

But he wasn't a husband. Not really. He was married, but being a husband meant something more. If he'd been a husband, he'd lift his new wife into his arms as the door swung open, he'd carry her over the threshold...

Devon moved past him into the marble-floored foyer.

"Is the entire house yours?"

The sound of her voice startled him. She hadn't spoken directly to him since the ceremony.

Ryan put down her suitcase and nodded.

"Yes."

"It's...it's very handsome."

He nodded again. "Thank you."

"How many rooms does it have?"

He had to think about that. Did it have eight or nine? It all depended on whether or not you counted the gym in the basement.

"Nine," he said, frowning. What in hell was the matter with him? he thought as he tossed his keys on the hall table. He wasn't a rental agent, showing the place to a prospective client.

It was just that it was weird, having her here, knowing she was actually going to live here—for a few months. He had lived in this house for seven years. In all that time, he had never shared it with anyone. Women came and women went; some of them spent a night, maybe two. Once in a great while—a very great while—he let a woman spend a long weekend.

But he'd never let one move in. Hell, he'd never let anybody move in, not even a housekeeper. Housekeepers, cleaning ladies, caterers—none of them were live-ins.

Ryan didn't like sharing his space.

Now, he'd contracted to share it with Devon, and for six entire months.

A thin trickle of sweat beaded on his forehead. How come he hadn't thought of that? He'd been so damned busy convincing her to go through with the marriage that he'd never given a thought to the logistics of it.

How would it be, sharing the breakfast table? Eating dinner with her? What would it be like, arguing over what TV program to watch or if the thermostat should be turned up or down? What would she say when he stayed late at the office, or met Frank for drinks instead of coming home after a long day? Would she bitch about dinner getting cold, or that he'd spoiled her plans for the evening when he hadn't known she'd even had plans for the evening?

Theirs was not a real marriage; she wouldn't have the right to complain about anything he did or didn't do. He should have made certain she understood that in advance.

"Where's the kitchen?"

He looked at her. She was standing in the center of the foyer, just under the big Orrefors crystal chandelier. Soft rays of light fell across her, turning her hair to silver. Spun silver silk, he thought, and his fingers curled against his palms.

"Ryan? There is a kitchen, isn't there?"

"Of course." He cleared his throat. "It's down that hall."

"Good." Devon smiled. "I thought I'd make us some coffee."

So, it was beginning. Not wanting to marry him was one thing but now that she had, she was going to go through the motions of being a wife.

"Fine. Coffee might be a good idea. We need to talk about—"

"—the ground rules," Devon said. "I agree."

She set off at a brisk pace, never pausing until they reached the kitchen. Devon threw on the light switch and looked around her. Ryan waited for her to gush over the size of the room and the multitude of up-to-the-minute appliances—Sharon certainly had—but Devon didn't even blink.

"Where do you keep the coffee?" she said.

"In the freezer." Ryan eased himself on to a high stool at the marble-topped counter. "The coffeepot's on that shelf."

He watched her as she measured the coffee into the filter. Her movements were brisk and efficient and when the coffee was finally ready, he tried not to smile as she filled two mugs and handed him one. He knew she was waiting for his response; for some reason, women seemed to think making a good cup of coffee ranked as one of life's great mysteries.

"Is it OK?" she said after he'd taken a sip.

"It's fine," he said, and he let the smile come. "Not quite as good as mine, but I suppose that's because you're not familiar with this particular filtering system."

Devon smiled politely. "No. No, I'm not."

"Well, I suppose you'll get used to it."

"Oh, I'm sure I will. Not that it matters." Her smile sweetened. "The coffee tastes fine to me, and this is probably one time in a million I'll be making it for you."

Ryan's brows drew together. "Well, of course, I have a housekeeper, but she generally doesn't come in until ten—"

"If you think I'm going to be doing kitchen duty," Devon said pleasantly, "you'd better think again."

Oh, how wonderful it was to see the wind go right out of his sails! She had waited for this moment ever since he'd taken her in his arms and kissed her right after the ceremony. Until that kiss, she'd gone through the week feeling sickeningly sorry for herself.

But that was over now, thanks to him. That kiss—that very public display of macho intent—had changed everything.

What did he think he'd acquired today? A woman to play at being wife for six months? One who'd cook his meals, iron his shirts, sleep in his bed? He'd never coerced a woman into his bed, he'd said, but he'd never mentioned how many he'd seduced into it.

That kiss had shown his true intentions.

She'd been so stupid, not hammering all the details out in advance. But they'd hammer them out now, and to hell with the consequences. She wasn't going to let herself be pushed around anymore.

"I didn't expect you to," he said with a frosty smile. "I told you, I have a housekeeper. As for breakfast coffee, I'm quite capable of making my own."

"How nice for you."

Ryan's eyes narrowed. "And," he said coldly, "while we're on the subject of how things are done around here, I suppose you should be aware that I often work late at my office."

She nodded. "Thank you for telling me," she said politely.

"And Frank and I usually have a drink together on Friday evenings."

"Sounds like fun," she said, even more politely.

"I go away for a couple of days on business with some frequency."

"Mmm. I'm sure you lead a busy life."

The desire to grab her by the shoulders and shake her until her teeth rattled was almost overwhelming but he had the feeling that would be playing right into her hands. Ryan forced himself to take a calming breath.

"So? What about you?" he asked.

Devon's brows lifted. "What about me?"

"Is there anything I should know about your comings and goings?"

"I can't think of a thing."

"About your friends?"

"Nope."

"You mean, you won't be going anywhere with anyone?"

Devon laughed. "Don't be silly. Of course I will."

Ryan's face darkened. "Dammit, that's what I just asked you. I've just explained my schedule. Now I'd like to hear yours."

"Why?"

"What do you mean, why? Because...because it's the civilized thing to do."

"I don't agree. Laying out your schedule was your idea, Ryan. I didn't ask how you spend your time and I don't expect you to ask about how I spend mine."

She had gone too far. She saw it in his face the second before he covered the distance between them, but short of shrinking back against the counter—and she'd have faced down a tank before giving him that satisfaction—there was nothing she could do about it.

His hands closed like talons on her shoulders. Despite herself, she gave a little gasp as he yanked her onto her toes.

"What nonsense is this, dammit? You are my wife, and I expect you to show me the proper respect."

"I am your partner in a six-month leasing arrangement," Devon answered. Her heart was tripping wildly but somehow she managed to keep her voice cool and steady. "I will not do anything to embarrass you and I expect you to show me the same courtesy. I will also put up whatever necessary front you require for the benefit of your grandfather. Other than that, I don't wish to have anything to do with you. Is that clear?"

A muscle knotted in Ryan's jaw. "You've thought this out pretty carefully, I see."

Devon stared into his cold eyes. She hadn't been thinking at all, not until just a little while ago, but why would she ever tell him that?

"Of course," she said.

Of course. Of course.

The words echoed in Ryan's head. How could she be so damned calm and collected when he was—when he was...

His hands tightened on her. There were ways to wipe that remote, faintly amused look from her face. He could give in to the urge to shake her like a rag doll.

Or he could press his mouth to hers and kiss her until she pleaded for mercy, until she wound her arms around his neck and begged him to take her, right here on the gleaming white floor. He would rip off her clothing and bare her body to his hands and make love to her until she sobbed out his name and begged him never to leave her.

With a muffled curse, he let go of her and took a step back.

"There's a guest suite on the top floor," he said tonelessly. "It has its own bathroom and small sitting room. I'm sure you'll find it satisfactory."

Devon nodded. Her heart was still pumping crazily, her shoulders ached where his fingers had bitten into her flesh, but she was determined to show no reaction.

"I'm sure I will," she said, and she strode from the kitchen.

It wasn't easy, getting her suitcase up the stairs and down the hall, but she managed.

Once inside her rooms, with the door safely locked, she breathed easier.

Her quarters were more than satisfactory, they were elegant. Under other circumstances, she'd have viewed the marble fireplace, the four-poster bed and the garden below the windows with pleasure.

But these were not other circumstances. This was her wedding night, and she was spending it alone.

Not that it was a real wedding night. It was all a fraud. That was what she'd told Bettina when her mother had insisted on stuffing a white lace nightgown into Devon's suitcase.

"I certainly won't need that," she'd said, her mouth curling with distaste.

But she should have needed it. A girl's wedding night was supposed to be a wonderful thing.

And this one could have been. She could have spent the night lying in Ryan's arms. No matter how strong their dislike for each other, there was no denying the power of the sexual attraction between them. Even down in the kitchen, she'd sensed that the tightly restrained violence in him could just as easily have become fiery passion.

Devon gave a little sob of despair as she spun away from the window. She undressed quickly, pulled on an old flannel nightgown and crept into the big four-poster bed.

Six months, she thought as she drew the blanket to her chin, that wasn't so long.

But a night could last an eternity when it was your wedding night and you were spending it alone.

CHAPTER SEVEN

It was Friday, the start of the long July 4th weekend.

Ryan would have thought half of Manhattan would be on its way east to the Hamptons or north to Connecticut by now, but it didn't look that way, not as he pulled open the door to The Watering Hole. Judging by the blast of music and the press of bodies, the bar was doing Friday night business as usual.

Ryan peered over the heads of the crowd toward the bar. It was going to take half the damned night to reach it, he thought irritably. Didn't these people have anywhere else to be?

"Hi, there."

Ryan looked down. A petite brunette with chocolate-brown eyes, a pouty, crimson mouth, and enough cleavage to endanger a midget, was smiling at him.

Ryan nodded. "Hi."

"Crowded, isn't it?"

"That it is."

Someone jostled the brunette. "Whoops," she said, giggling as she fell against Ryan. "Sorry about that."

Ryan smiled. He doubted that she felt the least bit sorry. Her head was tilted back, her eyes were sparkling. Her hands were pressed lightly against his chest and so was most of that impressive cleavage.

She was going to make some man very happy tonight, but he didn't even feel a twinge of pain that it wasn't going to be him.

"Sorry, darling," he said, "I'm meeting somebody."

"Oh." Her smile grew even poutier. "Lucky somebody."

Ryan's lips twisted. "Yeah," he said. He gave her a regretful smile, then worked his way past her, through the jammed room and to the bar.

He spotted Frank dead ahead, perched on one stool while valiantly defending another. Grinning, Ryan came up behind him.

"Do you have any idea," he said, "what a lucky so-and-so you are to be spending the evening with me?"

Frank snatched his jacket from the stool and fixed Ryan with a baleful glare.

"It's bad enough I had to spend the last fifteen minutes threatening death and destruction to everybody who tried to steal this seat from me. You don't really expect me to bat my eyes at you and simper, do you?"

Ryan laughed as he sat down next to his friend.

"Sorry I'm late, old buddy. I got hung up at the office." He nodded his thanks as an ever-observant Harry set his usual drink before him. "So," he said after a long swallow, "how's it going?"

Frank shrugged. "Depends on what we're talking about. Business is fine. My love life's in the toilet."

"What happened?"

"Oh, I broke up with Emma."

"Was that your latest?" Ryan smiled. "I know you always tell me their names and give me a full description—"

"—but lately, you haven't been paying attention, pal." Frank sighed. "Yes, Emma was my lady of the month."

"What went wrong?"

"The usual. She began making noises about forever after." Frank shuddered dramatically. "We sure as heck don't want 'em to do that, do we?"

"No," Ryan said after an almost imperceptible pause. "No, we certainly do not."

"And how're things in your world? Still putting in lots of overtime?"

What he was putting in, Ryan thought, was lots of time just sitting in his office long after the workday had ended, but what was the sense in hurrying home?

If he got home before seven, he and Devon ended up having dinner together, she at one end of the long dining room table, he at the other. How was her day? he'd ask. She'd say it had been fine and how was his? And then they'd slip back into the same polite silence that had surrounded them since their quarrel the day of their wedding.

He frowned and cleared his throat. "Yes, I'm still working late. I—I find I can get a lot done at night, when people are gone and the phones aren't ringing."

Frank nodded. "Well, why not? There's no point in hurrying home." He looked at Ryan, a sly grin easing across his mouth. "Unless, of course, the situation's changed and you're making the most of having a temporary wife under your roof."

Ryan's eyes went flat. "What in hell is that supposed to mean?"

"Hey, take it easy. I was just wondering if the status quo was still the status quo, OK?"

The cold look eased from Ryan's eyes. "Sure," he said. "Sorry, Frank, it's been a rough week."

"That's OK, man. I know how it is."

No, Ryan thought, Frank couldn't possibly know how it was.

Frank didn't share a house with a woman who might as well have been a ghost. He'd never entered a room she was in only to have her smile politely and walk out. He'd never walked into the unexpected scent of her perfume lingering in a hallway. And he sure as hell had never heard the soft sound of her laughter when she was on the phone and then spent the next hours going crazy, wondering who in hell was making her laugh when he couldn't.

No, Frank didn't know any of that. And he didn't lie alone in his bed, night after night, his body on fire with the knowledge that the most beautiful woman in the world lay alone in hers, just up a simple flight of stairs....

"...the old man?"

Ryan cleared his throat. "Sorry, Frank. I missed that."

"I asked if you and Devon are still making the weekly pilgrimage to your grandfather's house—or have things slackened off after five and a half months?"

"Are you kidding? It's a command performance. He and Brimley expect us at one o'clock sharp, every Sunday."

"And the old boy's still hale, hearty, and happy?"

"Oh, yeah, he's doing fine." Ryan smiled. "He's crazy about Devon. And believe it or not, she's gotten fond of him, now that she's gotten to know him."

"So, what happens when your attempt at matrimony ends a week from now? It *is* gonna end, isn't it?"

Ryan downed half his drink. "Absolutely."

"So, what's Grandpa gonna say to that?"

"What can he say? I told him about the contract Devon and I signed, right from the start. I never lied to him, Frank. You know that."

"Yeah, but he's got to be hoping."

"Sure. But he's a pragmatist. He wanted me to try marriage and I did. If it doesn't work..."

"*C'est la vie*, as they say in Brooklyn."

Ryan laughed. "Exactly."

"Well, you can always point out that it's as much his fault as anybody's. He didn't really find you a proper wife, did he?"

"No," Ryan said after a minute, "I suppose not."

"There she was, a modern-day version of Miss Goody Twoshoes, all sweetness and light and oh-so-eager to please, and what happens? She turns out to be a nasty-tempered, cold-hearted, conniving bitch who looks hot but actually has all the sexual warmth of a refriger—"

Ryan reached for Frank so fast that after it was over, people around them couldn't agree on what had happened first. All anyone was sure of was that one second two men were talking quietly and the next, the tall, handsome one shot to his feet, grabbed the heavier one by the collar and slammed him back against the bar so hard that it shook.

"Watch your mouth," he snarled.

"Hey." Frank's mouth opened and shut like a fish's. "Hey," he squeaked, standing on the tips of his toes and clutching at Ryan's hands, "what's the matter with you?"

"That's my wife you're talking about, Frank. My wife! And you'd damned well better not forget it."

"OK, man, OK. Just let go, will you?"

The two men stared at each other, Frank's face red, Ryan's stark white except for the deep, dark rage blazing in his eyes.

Slowly, Ryan's iron-fisted grasp loosened. The darkness faded from his eyes and he let go of Frank's shirt.

"Hell," he mumbled.

Frank sank down onto his stool. The noise level around them picked up, then returned to normal.

Ryan sat down, too. His hand trembled as he lifted his glass to his lips and drained it dry. He put the empty glass down and looked at Frank.

"She's my wife," he said. "Devon is my wife. Do you understand?"

He was gone before Frank could answer, shouldering his way through the crowd, out the door and into the night.

Devon sat in the living room, an unopened magazine in her lap.

Another Friday night, she thought. Another evening of trying not to imagine Ryan out on the town with his bachelor buddy.

Devon frowned, put the magazine on the end table, and got to her feet. Not that it was any of her business. Whatever Ryan did had nothing to do with her. Except for a piece of paper with their names printed on it, he was as much a bachelor as his friend, Frank Ross.

The house was so quiet. She still hadn't gotten used to that. Whenever Ryan wasn't home at night—which was almost always—she found herself pacing from room to room. Sometimes, when she heard his key in the lock, her heart would begin to race and it was all she could do to keep from flying down the stairs—and . . .

But that was only natural. She'd never really lived alone. When she was growing up, she'd shared a succession of cramped apartments with Bettina. In boarding school, she'd shared a room with another girl and then, after she'd graduated, she'd gone halves on the rent of a furnished apartment that wasn't as big as her entire bedroom was now.

The phone rang, startling her. Perhaps it was Jill, the model who'd tried to stop her from confronting Ryan that long-ago day at Montano's. They'd bumped into each other on Fifth Avenue a few weeks ago.

"What's new?" Jill had asked, and Devon had hesitated, then said that nothing was, really, and then they'd exchanged phone numbers. Jill was fun to talk to; she had a way of making Devon smile, and even, once in a very great while, laugh.

But it wasn't Jill phoning, it was Bettina.

"Hello, darling," she said. "I never can remember the time difference between New York and

California. Are you and Ryan in the middle of anything?''

Devon sighed. There was nothing subtle about her mother's questioning; only the phrasing varied from week to week.

"We're not in the middle of a thing, Mother. Ryan isn't even home."

"At this hour? Where is he?"

"Out with a friend, I think. I'm not sure."

"What do you mean, you're not sure? He's your husband."

"Mother, please. Must we play this game? You know Ryan and I don't have that kind of relationship. He lives his life, I live mine."

"That's no way to make a marriage work!"

Devon sank down on the sofa. It was hard to know what was more laughable, Bettina giving marital advice or Bettina pretending this was a real marriage.

Either way, Devon wasn't in the mood.

"Did you call for a specific reason, Mother?"

Bettina sniffed. "A mother doesn't need a specific reason to call her daughter—but as long as you asked, you might tell that husband of yours that this house is going to need a new water heater."

Devon sighed. "Ryan's not going to pay for the maintenance on that house forever, you know. Don't you think it's time you looked for a job?"

"He would," Bettina said crossly, "if you'd make that marriage work."

How could you make a marriage that wasn't a marriage work? Devon thought, her throat constricting.

"Ryan's a wonderful catch, Devon. If you play your cards right, you can keep him."

Devon gave a sharp laugh. "You make him sound like a fish!"

"Is he difficult to live with?"

Devon thought of how days could pass without them exchanging more than a polite "good morning" and an equally polite "goodnight."

"No," she said softly, "no, he's not."

"What's the problem, then? Don't tell me he's stingy!"

Stingy? Devon pictured the endless charge cards in her wallet—cards she never used. She thought of the untouched sums deposited weekly into her checking account, of the trust account she'd never touched....

"No, Mother. Ryan's very generous."

"He doesn't expect you to cook or clean, does he?"

Devon smiled for the first time. Cooking and cleaning were Bettina's idea of how the world would end.

"He has a housekeeper, and a cleaning service," she said.

"What's the problem, then?" Bettina's voice sharpened. "Aren't you doing what you can to please him in bed?"

Devon's cheeks went scarlet and she came quickly to her feet.

"I have to go, Mother," she lied. "I think I hear Ryan at the door now."

"That's it, isn't it? It's a sexual problem. Devon, you cannot behave like a prude if you want to keep a virile male like Ryan happy. Lose your inhibitions. Rent some videos. Buy some sexy lingerie. Men love black silk and garters and high-heeled shoes.''

"Goodbye, Mother," Devon said hurriedly. "I'll talk to you soon."

Her face was flaming as she hung up the phone.

Terrific. Just terrific. Marital advice from a world-class expert with some sex education thrown in free.

Why hadn't she ever told Bettina the truth, that she and Ryan didn't sleep together?

Because Bettina would have laughed in her face, that was why. She'd have called Devon every kind of fool for not sharing the bed of a man as handsome and sexy as Ryan Kincaid.

But he was more than handsome, more than sexy. He had a wonderful sense of humor. Devon had stumbled across him joking with the housekeeper one morning, Mrs. Cruz's lilting voice rising in laughter along with his as they teased each other in what was obviously a time-honored routine.

"Your 'usband," Mrs. Cruz had said with a girlish giggle that made her seem twenty years younger and forty pounds lighter, "he is some fine man, no?"

It was an opinion Mrs. Cruz seemed to share with the cleaning lady and the proprietor of every shop in the neighborhood.

According to all of them, Ryan was wonderful. His grandfather thought so, too; Devon could see the pride and love in James's eyes whenever he looked at Ryan, and who could blame him? When he was with the old man, Ryan was loving and warm and caring.

He was that way with everyone, except for her. And that was fine. It was just fine. Let the rest of the world be fooled; she knew the truth. She knew that Ryan was—that he was...

"What shall I do?" Devon whispered in despair, burying her face in her hands.

After a moment she wiped her eyes and got slowly to her feet. Another week, that was all she had to get through, and then this charade would be over. Seven days of living in Ryan's house, and then she would never have to see him again...

... *never have to pretend his homecoming didn't thrill her, especially on the few nights he came home in time for them to dine together, or to mask her pain when he didn't, when the hours ticked away and there was no key in the lock and no footsteps on the stairs.*

How many nights had she lain awake, listening for the sound of those footsteps? Wondering what she would do if they came up that last flight of steps, to her door?

Devon jumped to her feet. What was the matter with her tonight? She felt as if she were going crazy. She had to do something or she *would* go crazy.

A walk. A walk would burn off energy.

But it was Friday. The sidewalks would be crowded with couples going out for the evening. Their hands and arms would be linked, they'd be smiling at each other with their hearts on their sleeves.

All right, then. She'd go down to Ryan's gym, turn on the motor in the lap pool. It was one of the few things in the house she felt no guilt in using. In fact, she'd come to love the force of the water and the silken power of it against her skin—but she'd made it a point to only use the pool during the day, when there was no danger of Ryan finding her in it.

He'd been very polite and specific, telling her she was free to make full use of all the facilities in the place, but somehow the thought of having him see her in a bathing suit, however modest, was disturbing.

That was why she'd never used the pool at night.

But surely she'd be safe, using it now. It was barely seven o'clock; Ryan would surely not be home much before midnight. He never was, on Fridays. Devon always found herself lying in the dark, listening for his key in the lock, wondering where he'd been and who he'd been with.

Before she could think any more stupid thoughts, Devon went to her room, changed into a simple white maillot, then made her way down to the lap pool.

Ryan unlocked the front door and dropped his keys on the hall table.

"Devon?"

His voice echoed through the silence of the foyer.

"Devon? Are you here?"

Ryan scraped his hand through his hair as he went from room to empty room. All through the taxi ride home from The Watering Hole, he'd felt a tingling sense of anticipation at the thought of coming through that doorway and seeing Devon.

Now, anticipation was rapidly giving way to disappointment as it struck him that he was alone in the house.

Devon wasn't here.

Perhaps he should have called her, told her he'd changed his plans and would be home.

But he never called her, never told her whether he'd be home or not. He was either there or he wasn't; that was how it had been from the start. He had not just wanted that, he had demanded it.

Besides, what would he have told her? That he was coming home because he'd made an ass of himself with Frank? That he'd gotten pissed off at the things Frank had said about her when they were the very same things he, himself, had said and thought?

His footsteps echoed hollowly as he trotted up the marble steps to the second floor. He took a quick look into the library, into the music room and the game room.

They were all empty, as he'd known they would be.

Beyond, the stairs that led to Devon's rooms disappeared into the shadows. Ryan moved toward them. His hand closed around the banister; he tilted back his head and looked up at her closed door.

Was she up there? That was where she spent most of her time, when he was home; he could sometimes hear the sound of music drifting down from the CD player in her room. He knew her tastes by now: she favored Gershwin or Rachmaninoff. He smiled, thinking that until Devon had come along, he'd never thought anything written before the sixties was worth listening to and yet now...

But there was no music coming from her rooms tonight. For all he knew, she might be out. It was early, the night was soft and the sidewalk cafés were

open. She might have gone for a walk or to meet
a friend—to meet whoever it was she sometimes
laughed with on the telephone.

Ryan blew out his breath. What was the matter
with him tonight? So what if Frank had made a
few cracks about Devon? So what if he'd come
tearing home with some crazy idea that she'd smile
when she saw him, smile and...and—

And what? Ryan snorted in self-disgust. She was
probably as happy as he was that only a week remained until they could agree that there was no
point in even considering the renewal of their
contract.

What he'd told Frank was damned well the truth,
he thought as he headed down the stairs again. It
had been a long, rough week. What he needed right
now was some heavy-duty relaxation to ease the
kinks out of his muscles—and out of his head.

Ryan tossed his jacket and tie aside. A half hour
on the Nautilus, he told himself as he undid the
buttons on his shirt. Hell, an hour on the black
monster and then a workout in the lap pool would
fix him up fine.

He opened the door that led down to the gym
and frowned. Had he left the lights on down here
this morning? he wondered as he trotted down the
steps. And what was that noise? He must have left
the mechanism for the pool on, too.

He pushed open the door to the gym and his
breath caught in his throat.

Wisps of hazy steam rose like fog from the heated
water of the pool. And rising out of that mist, like
a water nymph stepping out of some timeless
legend, he saw Devon.

Ryan's gaze flew over her. Water beaded on her creamy skin, winking like diamonds in the light. Her hair, streaming down her back, was like a cascade of white-gold. Her body, encased in a simple white bathing suit, was barely hidden from his eyes. The water had turned the fabric translucent; there was no mistaking the firm thrust of her breasts or the crowning buds of her nipples and there was the faintest hint of a shadow at the juncture of her thighs.

And yet it was her face that captured him and made his heart begin to race. What held him transfixed was not the shock that widened her eyes or the stunned parting of her lips; it was the look of sheer joy that swept across her beautiful features in that one, unguarded instant when she saw him standing in the doorway.

"Ryan." Devon's voice was husky. "Wha...what are you doing here?"

He had to work his throat before he could speak. "I—I canceled my plans for tonight," he said. "I wanted to...to see you."

Devon licked her lips nervously. "I—I wouldn't have used the pool if...if I'd known that you were... Look, just let me towel off and change, and—"

"No."

"Ryan, please—"

The words died in her throat as he started slowly toward her. Her legs felt as if they had gone boneless. And she was trembling.

He was so beautiful, so magnificently male. His shirt was open almost to the waist, revealing a tanned, hard-muscled chest covered with a swirl of black hair. His eyes—his eyes were darker than she had ever seen them, and glowing with fire.

He stopped when he was inches away. "Devon," he said huskily.

"Don't," she whispered, "please, don't..."

And then she was in his arms, lifting her face blindly to his.

His mouth was hot, demanding everything with such intensity that she knew she should have been frightened.

But how could she fear what she had spent so many nights dreaming of? The feel of his lips against hers. The thrust of his tongue. The nip of his teeth.

Devon whispered his name as she wound her arms tightly around Ryan's neck. Her hands burrowed into the silken hair at the nape, swept under his shirt and across the powerful muscles in his shoulders and back.

"Yes," he said against her open mouth, "yes, sweetheart, yes."

He groaned and crushed her body to his. He could feel her heart race against his; he could feel the rounded sweetness of her breasts crushed against his chest. His body was alive to every inch of hers, to the long, exciting length of her legs and the upward tilt of her pelvis as he cupped her bottom in his hands and lifted her into the cradle of his hips.

"So long," he murmured as he rained hot kisses down her throat. "I've waited so long to do this." His hands swept up into her hair, framing her face, raising it to his so he could look at her flushed cheeks and glowing eyes and know that this was real, that she wanted him with the same fierce need as his.

"Ryan." Her voice was a whisper, a sigh against his lips. "Ryan, please. I want— I want..."

He swept her up into his arms, his mouth never leaving hers, and carried her up the stairs, up and up through the silence and the darkness to the deep softness of his bed.

Her bathing suit peeled away in his hands, leaving her trembling and naked in his arms. He tore off his own clothing, then came down on the bed beside her.

She was so beautiful. He drew back so he could see her: the high, rounded breasts, the curve of her waist, the womanly flare of her hips and the pale crest below them that he had waited so long to claim.

He wanted everything. Everything. He wanted to touch her, to run his fingertips over her skin and learn her body with his hands. To kiss her everywhere until the taste of her would become part of him.

Most of all, he wanted to bury himself deep in her heat and her softness.

"Devon," he said, his voice unsteady. "Devon..."

He took her face in his hands and kissed her mouth until it opened to his. His tongue swept over her lips and touched hers; her response was tentative and then he felt her tremble and the tip of her tongue darted into his mouth.

He was ready to explode. He had never wanted a woman so badly.

But he would wait. He would wait if it killed him, not just to prolong the ecstasy but because he could sense something beneath Devon's passion, a hesitation that almost made him think—that almost made him hope...

"Ryan?" she whispered, and the question and the need in her voice were almost his undoing.

He cupped her breast in his hand, rubbed his thumb over the nipple.

"Such perfect breasts," he said thickly. "So sweet..."

He bent his head to her, licked the beaded tip, then drew her flesh into his mouth, taking fierce pleasure in the sharp intake of her breath when he did. She was sobbing in his arms now, moving blindly against him, her body as pliant as quicksilver.

She tensed when his hand slipped over her belly; her fingers curled over his but he hushed her, kissed her eyes and her mouth and her throat and then, very slowly slid his hand down to the soft curls that hid her feminine heart. A fierce exaltation swept through him when he felt the dampness of those curls. He was trembling now, too, as he opened her, spreading the petals of her labia gently with his fingertips.

He touched her softly, slowly, moving his finger against her swollen flesh until her hips arched toward him and she was calling out his name.

Then, finally, he rose above her and knelt between her thighs.

"Devon," he said, "look at me."

And when she did, he leaned forward and entered her, filling her slowly... until he encountered that tiny bit of flesh he had only moments before let himself imagine he might find.

Imagining was one thing. Reality was another. The shock of the fragile barrier against the tip of his penis almost undid him.

He started to pull back—but Devon stopped him, her hands drawing his hips forward, her body arching toward his.

"Don't leave me now," she pleaded. "I'd die if you left me now, Ryan, I'd die."

I'd die, too, Ryan thought. Die at the thought of being without you, of never having said—of never having said...

He slipped his hands under Devon's hips, lifted her to him, and buried himself fully in the sweet, softly yielding body of his wife.

CHAPTER EIGHT

DEVON lay in the warmth of Ryan's arms, softly sated with passion...

And almost breathless with love.

She thought of all the weeks she'd been married to Ryan, living in the same house with him and telling herself she hated him.

It would have been laughable, had loving him not been so dangerous. How much safer her heart had been before tonight!

It was hard to remember that she'd once seen him as stubborn or arrogant or impossible. He was none of those things.

He was, instead, determined. Confident. Self-assured. Wonderfully, magnificently male. And he was funny, too, and bright and charming.

He was everything a woman could possibly want a man to be, and he was her husband—except he wasn't. Not really.

Unshed tears stung behind Devon's closed eyelids. What a stupid thing she'd done, falling in love when there was no future to it. She was a temporary part of Ryan's life; that was the way they'd both wanted it. The two of them had gone into this marriage with their eyes open.

That he'd made love to her changed absolutely nothing. He'd never made any pretense about wanting her in his bed. It was she who'd done all the pretending. Telling herself she despised him

133

when right now her heart was whispering that—in a way no scientist could ever explain—she had loved Ryan from the dawn of time.

Tonight, in one single instant, all her self-deception had been swept aside. It had happened when she'd stepped out of the pool and found him standing in the gym doorway, watching her.

The look on his face—that almost savage look of raw, uncompromising desire—should have set her heart racing with fear.

Instead, it had turned her bones to jelly.

She'd known what Ryan had to be seeing, that the water must have left her white maillot clinging to the contours of her body like wet silk. There was no way to disguise her reaction to him, either: the rapid rise of her breasts as her breathing quickened, the swift hardening of her nipples as her body responded to his.

Cover yourself, her brain had shrieked.

Let him look, her racing pulse had answered. Let him see what he does to you, let him know that you want him as badly as he wants you.

It was the very first time she'd dared admit the truth to herself. And, on the heels of that truth had come the stunning realization that somewhere between that first awful meeting at Montano's and now, she'd fallen deeply in love with Ryan Kincaid.

And she wanted him. Oh, yes, she wanted him with all her heart.

The air between them had seemed to shimmer with heat. The tension had stretched, until Devon could no more have prevented herself from going to him than she could have kept the sun from rising.

With a cry of surrender, she'd flown into his outstretched arms, lifting her mouth to his with all the pent-up hunger that filled her soul.

And he had met that hunger, met it and sated it, taken her from trembling innocence to the joyful fulfillment of womanhood in his arms.

Now, her joy was fading. She lay in the embrace of the man she loved and fought to keep from weeping.

Ryan had brought her happiness beyond imagining. And she had brought him pleasure. He had told her so, with his kisses, with the touch of his hands, with words that had thrilled her and made her blush.

But he hadn't said the simplest words of all, the ones that her heart ached for.

He hadn't said, "I love you."

Why should he? She was in his life by accident. He hadn't wanted her. He hadn't wanted a wife at all. Circumstance and honor had forced him into a marriage that wasn't a marriage—a marriage that would all too soon be over.

A sob rose in Devon's throat. Horrified, she bit down on her lip, but it was too late. The choked sound burst out anyway.

Ryan took her into his arms.

"Sweetheart?" he said. "What is it?"

She shook her head, smiling as best she could. "Nothing," she whispered.

Ryan knew it wasn't true. In the diffused light of the hall lamp, he could see the jewel-like sparkle of tears on Devon's lashes. He thought of that moment he'd penetrated her, of the delicate tracery of blood on her thighs, and he groaned with remorse.

"I hurt you," he said, his voice edged with guilt as he drew her closer. "Devon, sweetheart, I'm sorry. I didn't mean—"

"No," she said. "Oh, no, Ryan. You didn't hurt me." The warmth of his embrace, the joy of having him hold her close, brought a smile to her lips. "What happened was—it was wonderful."

He smiled back at her. "I'd have gone more slowly if I'd known. But I had no idea— I didn't expect—"

"That I'd be a virgin?" she said shyly, tracing the outline of his mouth with the tip of her finger. "Was I— Was it— Were you disappointed?"

"Disappointed?"

He thought of that moment when he'd realized that he was the first man to make love to her, the first she'd given herself to. Even thinking about it sent the blood pounding through his veins. He wanted her again, just as badly as he'd wanted her the first time, but it was too soon. Despite what she'd said, he'd seen the hint of pain in her eyes. So he contented himself with kissing her gently.

"How could a man be disappointed with such an incredible gift?" he said softly.

She blushed, and he could tell that his words had pleased her.

"I don't know," she whispered. "People say—I mean, there's something to be said for... for experience, isn't there?"

Ryan's gut tightened. People, hell, he thought. Only Bettina would offer such advice.

Dammit. Why would he think of Bettina now? She had been the reason Devon had gone into this marriage but she sure as hell hadn't had anything to do with Devon being in his arms.

What had just happened was their own private miracle.

"I don't see anybody in this bed but you and me," he said softly. "You were wonderful." He smiled. "As for experience—I'll be happy to give you all you want, I promise."

Devon smiled back at him, but her eyes were still solemn. "I suppose you thought—that you assumed—I mean, all things considered..."

"Forget what I assumed," he said gruffly, stroking her hair back from her still-flushed cheeks. "I can be a pigheaded jerk sometimes."

It pleased him to see the darkness in her eyes begin to fade.

"On the other hand," he said with a little smile, "I won't object if you try and persuade me that my self-analysis is faulty."

Devon laughed softly. "Well, I wouldn't call you pigheaded."

"You wouldn't?"

"No." She buried her hands in his dark hair, brought his face down to hers, and kissed him. "You're much too handsome to be compared to a pig."

Ryan grinned. "Thank you—I think."

He rolled onto his back, still holding her close. After a couple of minutes, he chuckled.

"What?" Devon said, lifting her head from his shoulder.

"I was just thinking about Frank."

"About Frank? How did he get into this conversation?"

"It's a long story, sweetheart. Let's just say I've been walking around like a powder keg with a short fuse for days and days. Frank happened to be the poor bastard that unknowingly lit it. He never knew what hit him when I finally exploded tonight."

Devon rolled onto her belly, folded her arms on Ryan's chest, and propped her chin on her linked hands.

"You quarreled with Frank? Is that why you came home early?"

"Yes. No." Ryan sighed as he looped his finger through a strand of her hair. "I was ticked off at Frank, yeah, but that's not why I came home early." He smiled at her as a tightness formed in his chest. "I came home because of you," he said, "because it was time to admit the truth to myself."

Devon's heart beat faster. "What truth?"

Ryan reached for her and drew her down into the curve of his arm.

"That I wanted to make love to you so badly I couldn't think straight anymore," he whispered. Her breath hitched as he stroked his hand over her hip. "All these months, telling myself I didn't want you, then lying in my bed each night, driving myself crazy imagining what would happen if I went up the steps to your room and took you in my arms..."

Color streaked into Devon's cheeks. "I—I imagined the same thing."

Bright green flame burned in the depths of Ryan's eyes. "Did you?" he said huskily.

"Night after night," she whispered.

He drew her close and kissed her until her lips were soft and clinging under his.

"No more separate rooms, sweetheart. No more separate beds. We've wasted too much time."

Yes, she thought, yes, they had, and now there was only one week left.

"You're mine," Ryan said fiercely. "Do you understand? You belong to me and no one else."

Forever, Ryan. Forever. Please, she thought, please, say the three little words that will make it so.

But he didn't say them. He moved instead, sliding down her body, until his mouth was hot against her belly. "Open to me," he whispered as he stroked her thighs apart.

"Ryan," Devon said in a broken whisper. "Ryan..."

And then his mouth was on her and she was lost.

They awoke early the next morning, still wrapped in each other's arms.

"Mmm," Ryan murmured, pressing his lips to her throat.

"Mmm," Devon sighed, tangling her fingers in his hair.

After long, sweet moments, Ryan sat up and slapped her lightly on the backside.

"Hey," Devon said indignantly.

"Hey, yourself," Ryan answered. He rolled from the bed, padded to the windows, and flung open the drapes. "It's morning, woman. Do you know what that means?"

Devon smiled and scrunched down under the blankets.

"Another twenty minutes of sleep?"

"Breakfast," Ryan said, striding back to the bed. He swept back the blankets, ignoring her shrieks, and scooped her into his arms. "Bacon. Eggs. Toast."

"Ryan! You put me down!" Laughing, Devon beat her fists against his shoulders as he hauled her into the bathroom.

"And buckets of coffee," he said as he stepped into the shower. Holding her firmly in the curve of one arm, he turned on the overhead and side sprays. "You've drained all my energy. I need food to restore my strength."

Devon turned in his arms, lifting her laughing face to his as the shower beat warmly down over their bodies.

"Is that all you need?" she said.

Her breath caught as Ryan's smile faded. "No," he whispered, his hands cupping her bottom. "No, my darling, I need much more than that. I need..."

He lifted her, his mouth finding hers as her legs locked around his waist, and then there was only the patter of the water and the sighs and murmurs of two people making love.

"So," Ryan said, "this is what New York is like on a holiday weekend, hmm?"

Devon looked up at him and smiled. They were in Central Park, strolling hand in hand through the Sheep Meadow. It was a hot, sunny day and the grassy field was alive with New Yorkers taking full advantage of the first long holiday weekend of the summer.

"What kind of question is that, coming from a native New Yorker?"

"Well, for openers, I'm not really a native New Yorker. I was born here but I went to live on Long Island, with James, when I was just a kid."

Devon nodded. "I know. I wondered about that. Did your parents die?"

"No, it was nothing as dramatic as that," Ryan said with a tight smile. "My mother decided it would be more exciting to traipse through jungles than to raise sons. And my father figured that with her gone, he might as well say to hell with responsibility and start enjoying *la dolce vita*."

Devon's smile faded. "You mean, they abandoned you?"

"It sounds a lot worse than it was, sweetheart. By then, I'd already lived more of my life with my grandfather than with my parents. They were forever going off somewhere—somewhere that didn't involve me."

"So you and Gordon both went to live with James?"

"Gordon was already away at college. He was twelve years older than I was."

"Mmm," Devon said. "You know, I wonder..."

"What?"

"Nothing, really. It's just that—well, one time, when I was home on vacation, Gordon asked me if I was happy being away from... from home. He said he knew another kid who'd been shunted off."

"You think he meant me?" Ryan asked in surprise.

Devon shrugged. "It's possible, isn't it?"

It was more than possible, Ryan thought slowly. It was absolutely logical; it would explain why Gordon had been so determined to provide for Devon, why he'd said he felt guilty about having neglected her.

I would never neglect her, Ryan thought suddenly. He watched as a soft breeze blew Devon's hair back from her face. She put up her hand and pushed it away from her eyes; it was the simplest of actions yet it somehow made his heart turn over.

Ryan laced his fingers through hers.

"What about you?" he asked.

She looked up at him and smiled. "What about me?"

"What was your childhood like?" He smiled. "I'll bet you were a solemn little girl with a sweet, shy smile."

"Well, the shy part is right." Her smile seemed tinged with sadness. "The only thing I really remember about my childhood is moving a lot, from San Francisco to Los Angeles, from Los Angeles to Reno and then to Las Vegas."

"Why?"

Devon shrugged her shoulders. "I suppose because my mother—because Bettina was always chasing after a . . . a better future. She was a waitress."

"A cocktail waitress," Ryan said.

"Yes." She looked up, caught by a certain flatness in his voice, and her expression grew defiant. "She did the best she could," she said. "Her choices may not have always been perfect, but it wasn't easy, raising a child by herself."

"And I'm sure she told you that, every chance she got."

"No! Well, yes. She did, but she was right. I mean..."

"Sweetheart." Ryan let go of Devon's hand and put his arm around her shoulders. "Forgive me. I wasn't trying to put you on the defensive. I just— I'm trying to imagine what it must have been like for you, shuttling from town to town, then being hustled off to a boarding school when Bettina married my brother."

Devon sighed and leaned her head against Ryan's shoulder.

"Actually," she said softly, "the boarding school wasn't so awful. Oh, it was stuffy. And silly. And the girls were horrible—they all knew each other, they came from the same backgrounds." She gave a little laugh. "They had names like Buffy and Muffy."

"And when they spoke, they sounded as if they had lockjaw," Ryan said, smiling.

"Exactly. But for all of that, I was happy. I went to bed and woke up in the same place each day, and at night I never had to worry whether or not the door was locked or what time Bettina would be home."

Or if she'd be home at all, Ryan thought grimly. His arm tightened around Devon. She'd never have to worry about anything again. Not ever. He would take care of her, he would cherish her and protect her.

"Whoever it was who said childhood was paradise," he said, trying for a light tone, "was obviously never a child."

Devon smiled. "Oh, I don't know," she said. "Those kids look pretty happy." She nodded toward two little boys running toward them with a fat cocker spaniel puppy trundling along at the end of a red leash. "And just look at that puppy, Ryan! Isn't he adorable?"

Suddenly the puppy broke free.

"Lady," one of the boys yelled. "Hey, lady, get the dog, would ya?"

Laughing, Devon ducked away from Ryan's encircling arm and set off toward the dog, which immediately decided this was a much better game than simply racing across the grass.

Ryan tucked his hands into his jeans, smiling as he watched Devon and the spaniel feinting right and left in their efforts to fool each other. It was a toss-up which was cuter, he thought, the girl or the dog.

His smile tilted. Hell, it wasn't a toss-up at all.

Devon wasn't just cuter. She was incredibly beautiful. Her face was devoid of any makeup, flushed with her exertions and bright with laughter. Her hair, loose at his request, floated over her shoulders like a silver halo as she danced around the puppy.

It was a joy to watch her, to see the graceful motion of her body, to know the lushness of it beneath the turned-up, baggy jeans she wore, jeans that were his, along with the equally oversize sweatshirt that drooped almost to her knees.

"What do you mean, you don't own any jeans?" he'd said in mock horror as they'd dressed this morning.

Devon had blushed and explained that the boarding school she'd attended had frowned on such things and she'd never felt comfortable, even after graduation, buying anything so frivolous.

"Frivolous?" he'd said incredulously, and he'd yanked a sweatshirt and a pair of old jeans he'd hoped might fit her from his drawer, tossed them at her and demanded she put them on.

She had, after first asking him to turn his back.

"Don't be silly," Ryan had said, folding his arms and hoping he looked totally unruffled by a display of feminine modesty that had charmed him right down to his toes. "You won't even know I'm here."

And she hadn't—not until the sight of her zipping up the jeans had been more than he could bear. With a soft groan, he'd decided breakfast could wait and he'd come up behind her, slipping one hand down into her panties and the other up under her shirt.

"Damn," he muttered. What a thing to be remembering now, in the middle of Central Park, especially since the memory was doing impolite things to his hormones.

Ryan tried to concentrate on something else. He watched as Devon snagged the puppy's leash and handed it to the two little boys. She turned and came toward him, and the sight of her, of that beautiful face and body, finished him off completely.

"Damn," he said again, and he sat down on the grass.

"What?" Devon said breathlessly as she collapsed beside him.

"Nothing," Ryan said with a grimace. He looked at her puzzled expression, laughed softly, and threw his arm around her shoulders. "I can't believe the effect you have on me. Here I was, thinking how great you looked in those jeans, and then I started thinking about what happened when you were getting into them this morning—and now I'm not fit to be seen by small children and fat puppies.''

"You're not fit to be..." Color flooded Devon's cheeks and she giggled and buried her face in Ryan's shoulder. "Are you serious?"

"Am I serious? she asks. Here I am, inches away from making a public spectacle of myself..." He laughed with her and then, unexpectedly, his laughter faded and died. "Devon? Did you ever have a moment when everything seemed to stand still? When you suddenly thought, I have never been happier than I am right now?"

Her breath caught as their eyes met. She wanted to tell him that she'd never felt anything like that until a little while ago, when she'd realized just how deeply she loved him.

"Yes," she said with a little smile. "Yes, I have."

Ryan nodded, his expression solemn. "It's how I feel this minute," he said, gently thumbing her hair back from her temples. "Everything is so...so damned perfect."

And, as their lips met, Ryan knew that the beautiful stranger who had lived in his home for five long months was a stranger no longer.

She was his wife, and he was deeply, passionately in love with her.

CHAPTER NINE

How did you tell a woman you'd fallen in love with her?

Ryan had never really given it much thought, perhaps because he'd never really imagined himself in love.

But if a man wanted to do such a thing, it would be a cinch. After all, what was so difficult about looking a woman in the eye and saying, Darling, I love you?

Plenty, as he was rapidly learning. For starters, just thinking of saying those words made him nervous. The corollary to "I love you" was "Come live with me and we'll be happy forever." And that was OK—except that after a lifetime of being convinced there was no "forever" when it came to men and women and affairs of the heart, who could blame him if he wanted to be sure everything was just right before he took that irretrievable last step?

Candlelight, soft music, long-stemmed roses were what he wanted, a very private, very romantic setting for what was going to be the most important moment of his life.

The Sheep Meadow in Central Park, on a hot July 4th Saturday with kites flying, radios blasting, and kids and dogs and people everywhere, was neither private nor romantic.

The little garden behind the brownstone was. Better still, he knew a restaurant just off 57th Street, a tiny, dimly lit place with wonderful French food and a marvelous wine cellar. Neither of them was really dressed for *La Salamandre* but its owner was an old friend. He'd not only welcome them warmly, he'd probably weep with Gallic joy once he realized his *bistro* was going to play an important role in such a romantic event.

Ryan got to his feet and held his hand out to Devon.

"Come on," he said, "let's go."

Her hand clasped his lightly. She stood up, smiled into his eyes, reached up and plucked a blade of grass out of his dark hair.

"Where are we off to?"

Ryan smiled back at her and put his arm around her waist.

"How does lunch sound?"

Devon put her arm around his waist, too. "It sounds fine. Did I ever tell you I make the world's best tuna melt on rye?"

"Tuna melt?" Ryan said, and shuddered.

"Ah, I see. The man doesn't go in for sophisticated foods." Devon grinned. "OK, then, how about bacon, lettuce and tomato on toast?"

"Well, I had something better than a coffee shop in mind."

"So did I. I thought we could go home and I'd..."

"Home?"

She looked at him. "Sorry," she said quickly, "I meant we could go back to...to your house and—"

"I liked it better when you called it 'home,'" Ryan said softly, brushing a kiss across her temple.

"But I want to take you someplace special for this particular lunch."

Devon smiled. "Where?"

He smiled, too, very mysteriously. "You'll see."

As they strolled out the Fifth Avenue exit and made their way slowly downtown, Ryan thought about what he'd say.

How did you tell your own wife that rather than divorcing her, you wanted to marry her all over again? With all the trimmings this time, the ones he'd snickered at over the years.

He wanted the whole nine yards: a church with sun streaming in the stained-glass windows, flowers at the altar and along both sides of the aisle. He wanted an organ playing—hell, he wanted violins and a cello and a choir. There'd be groomsmen and bridesmaids—but most of all, there'd be Devon, gliding toward him in a white lace gown and gossamer veil.

They'd take their vows and slip gold rings on each other's fingers. He'd given Devon a gold ring at that rushed little ceremony months ago but it hadn't meant much more to either of them than a cigar wrapper. The ring he'd give her this time would be one she chose, a perfect complement to the fiery diamond engagement ring she'd wear to proclaim his love.

Of course! That was how to do it. He wouldn't tell her he loved her now, not just yet. First, he'd buy her a ring, a diamond as beautiful and as flawless as she was. And he'd make dinner reservations at *La Salamandre*. Hell, he'd do better than that, he'd tell Alain he wanted to reserve the whole damned restaurant.

And when the moment was just right, he'd slip the ring from his pocket, take her hand in his, and say—

"Oh, Ryan, whoever would think we'd run into each other here?"

Ryan was so far away, happily lost in the imaginary world where he and Devon would begin their new lives, that at first he didn't even recognize the woman's voice, or her face.

But when she shrieked his name again, he blinked his eyes and brought her into sharp, unwelcome focus.

"Sharon," he said, and forced a smile to his lips. "How nice."

Sharon smiled at him as if there had never been a cross word between them the last time they'd seen each other, almost six months before.

"You look wonderful," she said happily. Before he could take a backward step, she flung her arms around his neck, rose on tiptoe, and planted a kiss on his lips. "But then," she said, laughing, "you always do."

Ryan's eyes met Devon's over Sharon's glossy head. He smiled uncomfortably and lifted his eyebrows.

Devon didn't react.

Well, that wasn't true. She *was* reacting; her silence, her frozen face—that was reaction enough. Ryan knew that much. It was the same way he'd seen women react in the past, when they decided they had a claim on his full-time attention.

But Devon *did* have a claim on his full-time attention. She was his . . . she was—

"Ryan, darling," Sharon purred, "aren't you going to introduce us?"

"Oh. Oh, of course." He took Sharon gently by the shoulders and put her at arm's length. "I, ah, I don't think you've met my... my..." Hell, what was the matter with him? Devon was his wife; it was a word he wanted to spend the rest of his life saying and here he was, choking over it the very first time he tried to use it. "Sharon," he said firmly, "this is Devon. My wife."

He held out his arm. Devon looked at it for what seemed an eternity before she moved forward and let him settle it around her shoulders. She smiled politely at Sharon.

"Hello," she said.

Sharon's smile was equally polite. "How do you do, Yvonne? It's very nice to meet you."

"It's Devon," Devon said politely. "And it's very nice to meet you, too."

"Your wife is so pretty, Ryan," Sharon said, turning up the wattage on her smile as she swung toward him. "Why have you been keeping her in hiding?"

"I haven't been. That is, I've been busy. Well, you know how it is..."

Damn. Damn! He was almost stuttering, but why? Sharon meant nothing to him; Devon meant everything. It was just that it was awkward, being confronted by your former lover with your... your wife at your side, especially when until fewer than twenty-four hours ago, you hadn't felt as if you had a wife at all.

"Ah, I see. It's Devonne who's been keeping you under wraps." Sharon gave a gay little laugh. "You mustn't do that, you know. We've all missed seeing Ryan around town.''

"I haven't kept him anywhere," Devon said, shooting Ryan a tight smile. "Isn't that right, Ryan?"

"Well . . . well . . ."

"Isn't that cute? The cat's got Ryan's tongue." Sharon batted her lashes. "Does she keep you on such a short leash, darling?"

"I don't keep him on any kind of leash," Devon snapped. "Actually, Ryan and I have a very modern relationship."

"Really," Sharon said, lifting her eyebrows.

"Really," Devon said, fighting a losing battle to keep her temper under control.

It was hard to know who she was angrier at, this . . . this overcoiffed, underdressed *femme fatale* or Ryan, standing like a big gorilla at her side.

How dare Ryan let this . . . this Sharon creature pull this disgusting act? *She* was his wife; why wasn't he acting as if she were?

But she wasn't his wife, Devon thought suddenly. A cold hand seemed to dig inside her chest and seize her heart. She wasn't his wife at all. She knew it, Ryan knew it—and, now that she thought about it, Sharon seemed to know it, too. It was the only reason she'd try this sort of routine.

"You know, sweetie," Sharon said, leaning closer, "you snatched this man right out from under my nose."

"Sharon," Ryan said, clearing his throat, "I don't think Devon is interested in—"

"He spent a weekend with me—well, of course there was nothing unusual in that, was there, Ryan?

You and I had spent dozens and dozens of weekends together." Sharon sighed. "And then, on Sunday, you said goodbye and that was that. A week to the day later, I opened the *New York Times* and read that you'd been married."

"Sharon," Ryan said, his voice sharp and chill, "we don't want to keep you."

"Oh, you're not keeping me, Ryan. Honestly, I'm so pleased to see you—and your lovely wife, of course. Lavonnne? Do ask Ryan for my number and give me a call. We'll get together, for lunch perhaps." She tossed back her mane of red hair and shot Devon a dazzling smile. "And we'll compare notes about Ryan. Won't that be fun?"

"Loads of fun," Devon said through her teeth.

Ryan's arm tightened around Devon's shoulders.

"Goodbye, Sharon," he said, and he urged Devon swiftly up the street. Hell, he thought, bloody hell. Heaven only knew what Devon thought now.

They stopped at the corner as the light went to red.

"Vicious bitch," Ryan muttered.

"I don't know why you'd say that," Devon said sweetly. "I thought she was very friendly."

Ryan snorted. "She's about as friendly as a cobra."

Devon glanced at him. His jaw was set, his mouth thin.

"She must have been very upset, reading about our—about your marriage that way."

The light changed to green, and she stepped off the curb, shrugging off Ryan's arm in the process.

"It wasn't the way she made it sound," he snapped.

"Wasn't it?"

"No, dammit, it was not! Our—relationship— had ended before you and I—before we—"

"Strange, that you never mentioned her."

"It isn't strange at all," Ryan said coldly. "I never asked you about any relationships you might have had before we . . . we signed our contract, now did I?"

No, Devon thought, he certainly had not. Why would he? Their marriage wasn't a marriage. Even now, after a night of incredible intimacy, neither of them could bring themselves to use the word.

Devon's throat constricted. Besides, what could he have said even if he'd wanted to say it? That there'd been a sexy, gorgeous woman in his life? That he'd been involved with her, right up to the minute his grandfather had forced him into a marriage he didn't want?

All these months she'd been so angry at Ryan, so angry at herself, so busy denying that she'd fallen in love with him . . . and not once, in all that time, had it occurred to her that Ryan might have left a woman behind when he signed his name to that damned marriage contract.

Oh, she'd assumed there'd been women who'd wept a bit when they read the announcement in the *Times*. A man as handsome, as virile, as Ryan would surely have had women.

But there was a world of difference between the singular and the plural of that word. "Women" were faceless, but this "woman" had not just a face but a name. She was a beautiful, sophisticated, sexy creature named Sharon who'd made her feel stupid and ugly.

"Listen," Ryan said brusquely, "just forget about Sharon, OK?"

Devon nodded. "Sure."

"Where do you want to have lunch?"

"Lunch?"

"Yes. Lunch. That's what we were going to do before we ran into Madam Viper."

"Actually, I'm not terribly hungry."

"I am," Ryan said grimly.

"Well, then…" Devon nodded toward a hot dog vendor on the next corner. "Buy yourself a hot dog, why don't you?"

"I am not in the mood for a hot dog from a pushcart," Ryan said irritably.

Damn Sharon, anyway! Ten minutes ago, he'd been strolling along with a sweetly smiling woman at his side, feeling as if he'd conquered the world.

Now he was stomping along Fifth Avenue with a fire-breathing dragon in tow. His euphoric mood seemed a thing of the far distant past.

Why had he let Sharon get away with all that crap? The sweetness-and-light routine, all that pretense about not getting Devon's name straight. It had all been bull. But he'd been so busy, trying to feel like a husband instead of a character in a bad farce, that he hadn't been able to do a damned thing about it.

And now Devon was putting on a jealousy act that was driving his blood pressure off the scale.

Ryan's eyes narrowed. OK, he thought. OK, let's have this out, here and now.

He jerked his head up, spotted a restaurant marquee down a side street, and grabbed hold of Devon's wrist.

"Where are we going?" she demanded.

"To have lunch," he growled, "and to talk, like civilized human beings."

Ryan hadn't chosen the restaurant so much as it had chosen him. The second he tugged Devon inside the door, he knew he'd made a mistake.

The place he'd unknowingly entered was one of Manhattan's newest, most exclusive restaurants. Ryan had been in it once and once had been enough. He was not impressed by pretention, and pretention was what this pocket of smoked glass, recessed lights, and overbearing waiters specialized in.

He was about to turn on his heel and walk out— but before he could do that, he caught the captain looking over him and Devon, all but sneering at their jeans, sweatshirts and sneakers.

Considering Ryan's mood, wild horses couldn't have dragged him out after that.

The captain approached, his face screwed up with distaste.

"Did you have a reservation, sir?"

Ryan looked beyond the tiny entryway. The restaurant was a sea of black leather booths, most of them empty.

"No," he said coldly.

"Ah, well then, I'm afraid—"

"Your restaurant is all but empty. I see no need for a reservation. We'll have a booth, please, and lunch menus."

"Sir, even if I ignored our reservation policy, you are not dressed—"

"Are you saying the lady and I have no clothes on?"

Devon bit her lip. "Ryan," she murmured, "really, I'm not hungry at all. Can't we just—"

Ryan's hand tightened on her arm. "Show us to a booth, please."

"Truly, I cannot."

"Truly, you can."

"Sir, I have already said—"

"I know what you said." Ryan's jaw thrust forward, his green eyes glittering dangerously. "And I know what I said. Now, what's it going to be, pal? A table? Or a little man-to-man chat?"

Color swept into the captain's face. He spun on his heel, marched them past several interested diners, and led them to a booth.

Devon kept her head up and her eyes fixed straight ahead until they were seated. Then she leaned forward and shot a furious look at Ryan.

"Are you incapable of behaving civilly?" she snapped.

"I am incapable of suffering fools gladly," Ryan snapped back. "Now, what do you want for lunch?"

"What are you so upset about, Ryan? I should think a 'man about town' like you wouldn't be the least bit put off by running into his mistress with his—with me at his side!"

"Sharon is not my mistress."

"Sorry. Wrong terminology. I meant to say your lover."

"She's not that, either. She told you, our relationship ended months ago."

"Yes." Devon smiled, but it felt as if there was a knife twisting in her heart. "Five months and three weeks ago, to be precise."

Ryan gave her a long, hard look. "Listen," he growled...

Two heavy vellum menus clattered onto the tabletop. Ryan looked up sharply. A waiter was standing over them, his face even more frozen than the captain's.

"Are you ready to order?"

"How could we be?" Ryan said through his teeth. "You only just delivered the damned menus—and by air express!"

"Ryan," Devon said, "please."

He took a deep breath. "OK. OK. Devon, what would you like?"

Devon shook her head. "I—I don't want lunch. I told you, I'd have been happy with a—"

"A hot dog," Ryan said.

The waiter recoiled as if he'd been struck. "Is that a joke, sir?"

"Do I look as if I'm joking?" Ryan's lips drew back from his teeth in a cold approximation of a smile. "The lady will have a hot dog. I'll have the same thing. On rolls, with mustard and sauerkraut."

"But—" The waiter's eyes met Ryan's. "Of course," he said stiffly.

Ryan took a deep breath after the man was gone. Hell, he thought, what was he so angry about? What was Devon so angry about? Damn Sharon anyway, for trying to stir up trouble.

He leaned forward across the table.

"Devon, listen to me. Sharon's not important. Let's forget all about her, OK?"

Devon hesitated. She wanted to believe him. But first, she had a question to ask. Every bone in her body told her not to ask it, but she could no more have kept it in than she could have stopped breathing.

"Ryan? Is...is that where you were?" she said softly. "All the nights you came home late, were you with her?"

Ryan looked as if she'd struck him.

"No," he said sharply, "of course not."

"I just—I just thought..."

"Thought what?"

He was furious. Furious! He had honored his marriage vows, dammit, even though Devon's cold dismissal of him had rendered those vows meaningless. Where in the hell did she get off, accusing him of infidelity?

"Thought what?" he repeated, his eyes cold. "That after months of forcing me to live like a monk, you suddenly had the right to ask me where I'd been spending my time?"

"I did not force you to live like a monk! You knew from day one that I had no intentions of— that our relationship would be...would be celibate. As for asking you where you'd been spending your time, Ryan Kincaid, even though I had the right to do that, I never once did!"

"What do you mean, you had the right?" Ryan's mouth twisted. "I've got news for you, baby. You signed on as my wife, not as my keeper."

"A man like you needs a keeper! A wife would have to be crazy to put up with your behavior, with...with you coming and going as you please and never an explanation or a phone call."

"You're damned right! It's a man's privilege to live his life as he chooses."

Not if he lives with a woman he loves, Devon thought desperately, not if he cares for her happiness.

"Not if he's married," she said.

"But I'm not married," Ryan snapped. "Remember telling me that? And you were right. I've got a piece of paper that says I wake up, free and unencumbered, in less than a week's time."

He saw the shock of his words register in her eyes, as soon as he'd said them. Oh, Lord, he thought, I've done it now. I'm a fool, a damned, stupid fool.

"Devon. I didn't mean—"

"Of course you did," she said.

Don't cry, she told herself fiercely. Dammit, Devon, do not cry!

"And I'm very, very grateful to you for bringing me back to reality." She slid toward the edge of the booth, a smile pasted to her lips. "Here I was, telling myself I could grit my teeth and get through the next week without screaming or tearing my hair out, but—"

"What the hell do you mean by that?"

"I mean that I have had enough."

Devon took a deep breath. Her heart was breaking but he must never know that. Never.

"For months," she said, "I have endured your bad temper and your arrogance, your ego and your vanity."

"You? You've endured? I've been the one who's had to endure, dammit!"

"Last night, just before you came home, Bettina phoned. She reminded me that . . . that it would be to her advantage, and to mine, if I could convince you to renew our contract. And so, last night, I decided even to . . . to—"

She cried out sharply as Ryan's fingers clamped, hard, around her wrist.

"Don't," he said. He spoke softly, but it didn't disguise the tightly contained fury coiled in every muscle of his body. "Don't say any more, Devon, I warn you."

She wrenched her hand from his and rose from the table, her back straight, determined not to let him see her pain or the depth and ugliness of her lie.

"Under the circumstances," she said, "I think you'll agree we can call the stipulations of our contract fulfilled and the term completed."

Devon turned, walked out of the restaurant, and out of Ryan's life.

CHAPTER TEN

"ARE you sure you won't have some more of that roast?" James Kincaid asked, smiling at Ryan across the dining room table. "Brimley may have outdone herself this evening, don't you think?"

Ryan looked up at Agnes Brimley, standing beside him, the usual look of prim disapproval in her eyes.

And well she might disapprove, he thought, his gaze settling on the serving platter in her hands.

Thick slabs of rare, well-marbled roast beef lay covered by a glistening sauce *béarnaise*. And why not? he thought wryly. The asparagus had been swimming in hollandaise, the potatoes had been adrift in butter.

What was roast beef and *béarnaise* sauce, compared to that?

"There's plenty for seconds," the housekeeper said brusquely.

Ryan smiled politely and shook his head.

"Thank you," he said, "but I've had more than enough."

More than enough was right, he thought as Brimley cleared the table. Mealtime at his grandfather's house had become one adventure in dining after another.

In fact, it had almost reached the point where Ryan would have been grateful to see a bowl of plain brown rice appear once again on the table.

Still, he thought, eyeing his grandfather as he went through his familiar after-dinner cigar ritual, the change in diet didn't seem to have done the old man any harm. If anything, James looked more robust than ever. He seemed that way, too. Lately, instead of announcing that it was his bedtime as the clock approached nine-thirty, he'd taken to settling in for a chat.

For three months now, the topic had been the same. Not, The World and How Much Better it Was Seventy Years Ago: James had given that up, along with Advice on How to Manage Kincaid, Incorporated, and the lecture that began with the words, "Time is passing," and ended with the admonition that Ryan was going to be thirty-three soon and it was time he settled down.

No, Ryan thought, his jaw tightening. No. Ever since July, when his contract with Devon had expired, the Kincaid Friday night chat had begun with the same half dozen words . . .

"Have you heard anything from Devon?"

Ryan looked at his grandfather. And there the words were, he thought, smiling politely. He shook his head and gave the response he always gave.

"No, sir. I haven't."

"Ah," James said. "No letters? No phone calls?"

"No."

"And you have not tried to contact her?"

"No, Grandfather, I have not."

James nodded. "Shall we adjourn to the library?"

Ryan sighed. Discussion ended, he thought with relief.

"Of course," he said. "Let me help you."

"No," his grandfather said briskly. "Thank you, but I can manage." He rose from his chair creakily but with surprising speed for a man who had recently passed his eighty-seventh birthday. "Ring for the old witch, will you, Ryan? Tell her to serve our coffee by the fireplace—and tell her she'd better have made that chocolate cream pie as I told her to."

Ryan's lips twitched. "I'll do that."

He made his way to the kitchen and delivered grandfather's request—a much more polite version—firsthand. By the time he entered the library, James was seated in his favorite chair. There was a glass of cognac in his gnarled hand.

"Pour yourself a drink, my boy, and come and sit with me." When Ryan was settled in a chair alongside, James cleared his throat. "Why haven't you?" he said.

Ryan frowned. "Why haven't I what?"

"Contacted her. Devon, I mean."

Ryan's frown deepened. This was a new tack.

"There's no point," he answered.

James looked at him. "A man's wife runs off and he thinks there's no point in getting in touch and asking why? The modern world is strange, my boy. Very strange."

Ryan sighed and got to his feet. "Grandfather," he said gently, "I think you may be a bit confused about the circumstances here. Devon didn't run off, she walked out. Calmly, coolly, and very deliberately. And I've told you the reason—"

"Yes, yes, you've told me. Because she didn't want to stay married to you any longer."

"And because I felt the same way." Ryan's mouth thinned. "She wasn't really my wife, Grandfather. Do you remember? I told you about the contract she and I signed. I told you about it before the wedding, and you said you understood. You said—"

"For pity's sake, Ryan, I am not senile. I know what you said and I know what I said." James's bushy white eyebrows knotted across the bridge of his nose. "I also know what any fool with half a brain can see. You fell in love with that girl, Ryan, and you are still in love with her."

Ryan flushed and put his glass of cognac down on the fireplace mantel.

"Don't be silly."

"I am never silly, young man."

"Look, Grandfather, I know you have this dream that I'll find the perfect woman, marry her, settle down and have kids but—"

"You did find the perfect woman," James said sternly. "And you let her slip away from you."

"The only thing 'perfect' about Devon was her acting ability."

"Nonsense. She adored you."

Ryan laughed. "She adored my money, you mean."

"Ryan, you are my flesh and blood and I love you—but sometimes I wonder if you didn't inherit your brains from your mother's side of the family. Adored your money, indeed! If that's the case, why hasn't she touched her trust account?"

"How should I know?"

"And her charge accounts—did you ever get around to canceling them?"

Ryan frowned. "She probably forgot she had them."

"Ah. Well, that would be logical, wouldn't it? This avaricious creature would certainly tend to forget she had unlimited credit and a fat trust account."

"Two," Ryan mumbled.

"What?"

"Two trust accounts. I, ah, I set one up for her myself. I thought—it seemed like the right thing to do."

"Even better," James said crossly. "She hasn't touched two trusts and who knows how many credit cards. Yes, that certainly fits the profile of a greedy female who married you for your money."

"She married me because it was what her mother wanted," Ryan said, his tone sharp. "Believe me, Grandfather, Devon showed a true daughter's devotion to her mother, right to the end."

"I'm sure that has some deep, dark meaning," James said testily, "but it doesn't hold water, considering that Devon's hardly had anything to do with her mother since she left New York."

Ryan's frown deepened. "How do you know that?"

"Bettina phoned me. She was all sniffles and tears."

"I'll bet. She wanted money, I suppose."

"She wanted to know what had happened here, to turn Devon against her. It seems the girl only drops her an occasional card and phones less frequently than that."

"What are you talking about? Why would Devon have to write her postcards when they both live in San Francisco?"

"They do not both live in San Francisco, Ryan. The girl lives somewhere else."

"Where?"

"How should I know?"

Ryan looked at his grandfather, his face grim. "Didn't Bettina tell you?"

"She may have."

"Grandfather, dammit, did she tell you where Devon lives or didn't she?"

The old man shrugged. "Chicago, I think."

"Chicago? What in hell is she doing there? What's she living on, if she's not tapping into the trust funds? Does she even know anybody in Chicago?"

James's eyebrows lifted. "Which question would you like me to answer first? Not that it matters. My answer is the same to all three. I've no idea. And, when one comes right down to it, why should you give a tinker's dam?"

Ryan's mouth opened, then shut. He turned away, busied himself pouring more cognac, then looked at James.

"I don't. I'm just—curious. After all, when our divorce is final, the papers will have to be sent somewhere. I thought, all this time, they could be sent care of Bettina, that Devon was—"

"That she was what? Living with her mother? Did you picture the two of them laughing up their communal sleeve at what a fool you'd been to have fallen in love with the girl?"

"Dammit, Grandfather, I did not do any such thing!"

"Well, I'm glad to hear it," James said mildly. "I'd hate to think you'd turned into a hermit because you were carrying the torch for your own wife."

"Carrying the..." Ryan laughed. "Where on earth did you get that idea?"

"Oh, from the fact that you've taken to coming here every Friday for dinner, instead of begging off so you can paint the town red with your friend, Frank Ross."

"I still see Frank. It's just that—look, there comes a time in a man's life when he's bored, playing around..."

"Your secretary says you stay late at the office nights and you spend half your weekends there."

"That's crazy," Ryan sputtered. "And besides, it's my business if I work late. What the hell right have you got to question Sylvia—and what right has she got to tell you how I spend my time?"

James smiled slyly. "She didn't. It was just a lucky stab in the dark."

Ryan glared at his grandfather. Then he began to laugh.

"You're a sly old devil," he said. "But you're wrong about Devon. I didn't love her."

"Didn't you?"

"No. Absolutely not."

"Well, that's a relief." James took the glass of cognac Ryan held out to him. "I was afraid you might go storming off to Chicago and make a fool of yourself when you found out she was seeing somebody."

"What?"

"I said—"

"I heard what you said, dammit! How can she be seeing somebody? She's still married to me."

"Technically, I suppose she is, but—"

"Who?" Ryan growled. "Who is she seeing? Did Bettina say?"

James sighed and leaned back in his chair. "How would Bettina know? I just told you, the girl hardly speaks to her."

"Well, then how do you know she's seeing somebody?"

"I don't."

Ryan went very still. "Excuse me?"

"I don't know," his grandfather said, and chuckled. "But I certainly got your dander up, didn't I, boy?"

"Dammit," Ryan said softly, "if you weren't my grandfather, I'd... I'd—"

"Stop blathering, Ryan, and try admitting the truth for a change. You fell in love with Devon and you're still in love with her."

Ryan glowered at the old man and then he sighed and dropped back into his chair.

"All right," he said softly. "If you must know— yes. I loved her. But she never knew. Thank God for that, anyway."

"You're pleased she never knew?"

"You're damned right I am!" Ryan shot to his feet, his temper at the boiling level. "Listen, you crafty old man, you'd better just stop playing God. Hell, you got me—and Devon—into one hell of a mess."

"Falling in love is never simple," James said.

"Simple? It's hell! How do you think I feel, knowing I fell head over heels for a woman who was playing me for a sucker?"

"Ryan. Ryan, my boy. What happened? You've only told me you quarreled the last time you saw each other, never what you quarreled about."

"Hell," Ryan muttered, slashing his fingers through his hair. "Hell, how do I know what it was about? She accused me of not having been faithful to her and I got angry and I said some things..." He took a deep breath. "I could feel the walls closing in. I know you don't understand, but—"

"Of course I understand," James said. "It's how I felt just before I proposed to your grandmother, sixty-three years ago." He laughed. "It's how I feel now, knowing I'm going to pop the question to that miserable old hag in the kitchen."

Ryan's eyes widened. "Brimley?" he said. "Are you serious?"

James smiled. "A man needs a good woman at his side, Ryan, one with spirit and determination, one who loves him enough to take his bad temper and throw it right back in his teeth."

"Devon scored in all those departments." Ryan's mouth thinned. "She also played me for a fool. She admitted—well, never mind what she admitted. The bottom line was that she'd only pretended to care for me in hopes of having me agree to extend our marriage contract."

"For what reason?"

"What reason do you think? For money."

"Ah." James nodded. "Of course. So she could have access to even more money she would never touch. Yes, indeed. That makes perfect sense."

Ryan shook his head. "Listen," he said gently, "I know what you're trying to do. And I'm grateful, Grandfather. Really. But... but even if I eliminate the profit angle, what happened that last day only proves she didn't love me."

"For instance."

"Well, for one thing, we bumped into an old girlfriend of mine." His mouth tightened. "Devon turned right around and accused me of cheating on her."

"Did she have any cause to think you'd been cheating?"

"Of course not. Sharon—the old girlfriend—put on an interesting performance, but—"

"Devon was jealous, then."

"Jealous? Why should she have been jealous?"

James smiled. "Perhaps because she loved you."

"Yeah," Ryan said. His smile twisted. "I tried telling myself that, but then she started snapping at me about how I'd been out nights and she'd never known where I was or what I'd been doing."

"Typically female, hmm?"

"Yes, dammit to hell. Typically!" Ryan slammed his fist onto the mantel. "And the hell of it is, I'd have sold my soul if I'd thought it would have made her really give a damn about where I'd been spending my time. Why couldn't she understand that no one mattered to me after I'd met her?"

"Women profess themselves to be the intuitive sex, my boy," James said gently, "but I have found that they need to be told certain things."

"If I'd thought for a minute that Devon wanted me near her, I'd have been home every night. She

was everything to me, Grandfather, everything I
ever wanted . . .''

Ryan's words drifted to silence. After a moment
his grandfather cleared his throat.

"Life is short," he said. "Before you know it,
you look around and it's all behind you. Find her,
Ryan. Tell her what's in your heart."

Ryan nodded. He wanted to say something but
his throat felt tight. He cleared it, hard.

"Thank you, sir. For everything."

"Nonsense. I'm an interfering old man. We both
know that."

A smile eased across Ryan's lips. "You're right,"
he said. "Which reminds me . . . I've been meaning
to ask you about that diagnosis your doctors sup-
posedly gave you all those months ago."

"Are you questioning my veracity, Ryan?"

"Yes, sir," Ryan said politely, "I most certainly
am."

His grandfather's eyes twinkled. "Everything I
told you was the truth. They said my time was
limited and that it would be wise to put my affairs
in order." James chuckled. "But then, that's the
advice any intelligent physician gives a man who's
staring ninety in the face, wouldn't you agree?"

Ryan tried to look stern but it was impossible.
After a moment, he began to grin.

"I'm counting on you to look one hundred in
the face, old man. What would my children do
without you around to make their lives miserable?"

The two men looked at each other and smiled.
Then Ryan put his arms around his grandfather and
hugged him.

"I love you," he said gruffly, and then he was gone.

Chicago was caught in the grip of an Indian summer heat wave.

The hot breath of the prairie had blown in over the city five days before and showed no signs of retreating. Each day, the temperature hit new highs and dispositions hit new lows.

Devon was definitely not in the best of moods.

During the night, the wheezing electric fan in the tiny bedroom of her all-but-airless apartment had given its last gasp and died, breathing out a wisp of acrid electrical smoke.

And now the air-conditioning system in Holdridge's Department Store had decided to do the very same thing. The store was rapidly turning into a sauna.

The customers were not fools. They fled. But the sales staff was trapped, and trapped in uniform.

And a stupid uniform it was, Devon thought irritably as she tried to straighten the sweaters that were piled on the men's boutique sales counter. A black suit, the pocket emblazoned with the Holdridge crest, a white blouse, stockings and medium-heeled leather pumps might make sense in midwinter.

On a day like this, with the AC only a memory, the outfit was simple torture.

The blouse—polyester, so it didn't breathe at all—was stuck to her skin. The suit—also polyester—was so wet it was clammy. And the miserable heat had made her feet swell so that every step in the pumps was agony.

No, Devon thought grimly as she folded sweater after sweater, her mood was not good. But then, it hadn't been good for a long time now, if the succession of roommates she'd gone through in the last three months was to be believed.

"Honestly, Devon," the last one had said just a few days ago, "if I were you, I'd go back and confront the guy that put me through the mill, and I'd either tell him I still love him or I'd sock him in the jaw. Maybe then you'd be fit for human company again."

"Nobody put me through the mill," Devon had snapped. "And besides, I never loved him and I already did sock him in the jaw."

She should have socked him again, Devon thought furiously. But she hadn't. Her roommate was probably right. Maybe that was the reason she was still so damned angry.

She'd been angry since she left New York, which she'd done an hour after she'd marched out of that stupid restaurant and out of Ryan Kincaid's even stupider life. She'd paused only long enough to stuff her clothes into her suitcase, then headed for the Port Authority Bus Terminal.

"I want a one-way ticket on the first bus heading out of the city," she'd said.

That was how she'd landed in Chicago. What did her destination matter? She had no place she wanted to be, only places she *didn't* want to be, like San Francisco. Like New York.

And Chicago was working out just fine. It was big, it was impersonal, she'd found a job and a place to live almost overnight, and pretty soon now, any last, unpleasant memories of Ryan Kincaid would be gone from her life forever.

It was just pathetic that she'd ever thought herself in love with him.

Devon made a face as she folded another sweater. In love with Ryan Kincaid?

"Ridiculous," she muttered, under her breath.

What she'd been in love with was the *idea* of being in love. It was lots more palatable than admitting the truth, that she'd wanted to go to bed with Ryan from Day One.

Well, she had. She had, and so what? Sex had turned out to be—to be fun. Yes, she thought, slamming another sweater into the stack, that was the word for it. Fun. All the rest—the magic and the mystery and the dizzying joy—had been products of her overheated imagination.

As for Ryan himself—if she ever saw him again, she'd—she'd do what that last roommate had suggested, she'd make a fist, haul back and hit him. Then maybe she wouldn't waste time thinking about him, seeing him in every tall, dark-haired stranger, hearing his voice...

"Good afternoon, miss."

Devon's heart turned over. She was doing it again, hearing Ryan's voice. Damn him, she thought, damn him.

"Miss? Could you help me, please?"

"No," Devon whispered, without so much as turning around. "No, I cannot help you." She cleared her throat. "I'm very busy, sir. Surely, you can see that."

"What I can see," the amused male voice said, "is that you are a very impolite salesclerk. I think I'm going to have to report you to the manager."

Devon took a deep breath. "Do it, then," she said, and whirled around. "Do it and be—and be..."

Oh, Lord.

It was Ryan. Ryan, tall and handsome and just as she remembered him.

"Bastard," she swore, and launched herself at him over the sweaters.

Laughing, he caught her in his arms, one hand pinning her wrists against his chest between them, the other tangling in her hair so that the pins that held it neatly at the nape of her neck tumbled to the floor and her hair came cascading down her shoulders.

"Uh-uh, sweetheart," he said. "You only get to punch me out once."

"You—you rat! You baboon! You—"

"Is that any way to say hello to your husband?"

Devon glared at him. "You are not my husband!"

"I sure as hell am. I've got a piece of paper in my pocket that says so."

"Ryan, dammit, let go of me!"

He grinned. "No."

Devon wriggled in his arms. "Let—me—go!"

Ryan's breath caught. "If you keep moving like that," he said softly, "I'm liable to toss you down on those sweaters and give you a much more graphic demonstration of our marital status."

Color flooded her cheeks. "What are you doing here? And how did you find me?"

"Bettina gave me your address."

"Bettina! You spoke to my mother?"

He nodded. "Yeah. Yeah, I did. She misses you, Devon. She almost has me convinced that somewhere beneath all the paint and sequins, there's a woman wanting to try to be a mother." Ryan buried his nose in Devon's hair. "Lord," he murmured, "I'd almost forgotten how wonderful you smell."

"You still haven't explained what you're doing here, Ryan."

"What do you think I'm doing here? I came to find you and take you home."

"I *am* home. I live in Chicago now."

Ryan smiled. "Your home is in New York, with me."

A faint tremor swept along Devon's skin. Don't, she thought, please, don't do this to me. Don't let me begin to hope.

"What's the matter?" she said. "Did your lawyers find something wrong with that contract?"

"What contract?"

"Don't play games with me, Ryan. You know very well what contract, and I'm warning you right now, I don't care what they found wrong with it. I lived up to my end and—"

"Actually, you didn't."

"I did. I had to put in six months as your wife, and I put in—"

"You put in five months, three weeks, and one day." He smiled. "I figured it out, darling. You owe me at least forty-three years more."

Devon blinked. "What?"

Ryan took her face in his hands and kissed her. She fought him at first, twisting her head from side to side, but he was persistent and oh, the warmth of his mouth was as sweet and wonderful as she'd dreamed night after lonely night since she'd left him.

With a little sob, Devon gave herself up to the kiss.

After a long, long time, he drew back, just far enough so he could look into her eyes.

"That's how long my grandparents were married," he whispered. "Forty-three years plus a couple of months, but I'm damned and determined to break that record."

"Ryan." Devon couldn't help it. Her voice broke; she could feel tears filling her eyes. "Ryan, don't do this. I—I don't understand what you want."

"You," he said. "That's what I want. I love you, Devon, I love you with all my heart."

"But . . . but you said—"

"I said a lot of things. And so did you."

Her face pinkened. "I know. But . . . but I was angry. And hurt. I didn't mean—"

"I didn't, either." Ryan stroked his thumb over her bottom lip. "I was going to tell you I loved you that day in Central Park."

"But . . . but why didn't you?"

He sighed and leaned his forehead against hers. "I don't know. A combination of wanting the right setting and sheer terror, maybe." He smiled and pressed a gentle kiss to her lips. "We confirmed bachelors are a special breed, sweetheart. We don't give up easily."

Devon laughed softly. "So I see."

"Anyway, there I was, spinning dreams in my head of a table for two, candlelight, music, a diamond ring that would shine like your beautiful eyes." He frowned. "And wham, bam, we walked right into Sharon."

Devon smiled tremulously as she linked her hands behind his neck.

"I hated her," she whispered. "She was so beautiful. So smug."

"She never meant anything to me, Devon. No one did, until I met you."

"Oh, Ryan, I love you so much."

Ryan kissed her, long and deep. Then he drew back and took a little box from his pocket.

"Open it," he said softly.

Devon did, with trembling fingers. An amethyst ring, as deep and dark as her eyes, the stone encircled by sparkling diamonds, winked back at her.

"Ryan? Oh, Ryan..."

"I thought I would buy you a diamond," Ryan said as he slipped the ring on her finger. "But all I could think of was that your eyes were more beautiful and more mysterious than any diamond."

"Miss Franklin! What is going on here?"

Devon gasped. "It's Mr. Nelson," she muttered. "The manager."

Ryan let her break free of his embrace but he kept one arm firmly around her shoulders. He smiled at the tall, thin man in the shiny black suit who was striding toward them.

"How do you do, Mr. Nelson?" Ryan extended his hand. "My name is Kincaid."

The manager took Ryan's hand cautiously. "Is there a problem here, Mr. Kincaid?"

"No." Ryan smiled. "No, there's no problem."

Nelson frowned and looked pointedly at Devon.

"Miss Franklin? Have you an explanation for your behavior?"

"Well," Devon began, but Ryan's voice cut across hers.

"The explanation's simple." His arm tightened around Devon's shoulders. "I've come to take my wife home."

"Your wife?"

"That's right. You see, Mr. Nelson, this young woman's name isn't Devon Franklin. It's Devon Kincaid."

Devon's heart filled with happiness. She smiled and looked into her husband's eyes.

"Actually," she said, "it's Mrs. Ryan Kincaid."

And then she was back in Ryan's arms, where she had always belonged.

EPILOGUE

"NINETY-FIVE candles on a birthday cake," James said irritably. "It's enough to burn the place down!"

Agnes Brimley Kincaid shot her husband a look of disapproval.

"Blow out the candles, James, and be quick about it, please." Her stern face softened as she looked at the child in Ryan's arms. "Little Jamie wants a bite of birthday cake, doesn't he, snookums?"

Little Jamie, eleven months old and as beautiful as any baby had ever been, bounced with delight. Ryan shifted his son's considerable weight and tried to sound stern.

"You're spoiling him, Agnes," he said.

Agnes Kincaid leaned toward her step-grandson, widened her eyes, waggled her hands behind her ears and blew a noisy gust of air over her pursed lips. Little Jamie crowed with laughter.

"Is dat what gram-mums is doing to her pwecious widdlle man?" she asked in a singsong lisp.

Ryan's eyes met his grandfather's over Agnes's gray head. The two men grinned at each other, and then James leaned forward, took a deep breath, and blew out all the candles on his cake.

"There," he said, "it's done, and I'll probably die of cardiac arrest in the next thirty seconds."

"Complaints, complaints, complaints," his wife said crossly, but she turned away from the baby, bent down and kissed her husband soundly on the mouth. "Happy birthday, you old curmudgeon, and many, many more."

"Nonsense," James grumbled, but he smiled.

Little Jamie, ignored for more time than he deemed appropriate, gave a shriek of laughter and sank one chubby fist into his father's dark hair.

"Ouch," Ryan said. "Hey, kid, show some respect for your old man, huh?"

"Jamie, you devil!" Devon Franklin Kincaid tried not to laugh as she came through the door from the kitchen with a bowl of home-made ice cream in her hands. "What on earth are you doing to your daddy?"

"Making me bald before my time," Ryan said, wincing. "See what you can do about separating my son's fingers from my head while leaving some of my hair behind, will you please?"

Devon put down the ice cream and came toward her husband.

"Our son, you male chauvinist," she said, smiling. "Here, bend down a little and I'll see what I can do."

Ryan cocked his head toward his wife's as she rose on her toes and worked gently at easing their child's death grip on his hair. She was so beautiful. So incredibly beautiful. Even after eight years of marriage, the sight of her was enough to make his heartbeat quicken.

"Still calling me names, Mrs. Kincaid?" he said softly.

"Only when you deserve to be called them," she answered saucily. "There," she said. "How's that?"

"My scalp hurts," Ryan said, lying through his teeth. "You'll have to give me a kiss to make me feel better."

Devon smiled and looked into the eyes of her handsome husband. How could a woman still feel this way, after eight years and two children? But she did. Sometimes, when she looked up and saw Ryan entering a room, her heart felt as if it were going to leap from her chest.

"Gladly," she whispered.

"Right here," he said, tapping his finger lightly against his lips. "Smack on the kisser."

She smiled and brushed his lips with hers.

"That," Ryan said softly, "is not a kiss."

"Eeew," a voice said, "aren't they icky?"

Everyone laughed as a little girl with Ryan's black hair and Devon's amethyst eyes came bursting into the room.

"Are you and Mommy done being icky?" she said impatiently. "'Cause if you are, Daddy, you promised you'd come and help me look for frogs."

Ryan handed the baby to Devon and squatted down beside his five-year-old daughter. Her hair was tousled, there was a smudge of dirt on her chin, and as he looked at her, he thought with a fierce pang that she was going to grow up to be every bit as beautiful as her mother.

"I will, baby. But right now, I want you to go wash your hands and face."

Susannah Kincaid, who had been named for her paternal grandmother, gave her father a rebellious glare.

"Why?"

"Well, because you have to," Ryan said reasonably, "especially if you want a slice of Grandpa's birthday cake."

His daughter hesitated. Ryan could see her need to assert herself silently warring with the knowledge that neither her father nor her mother would tolerate much nonsense before gently lowering the boom. It was hard not to smile. His daughter was like a miniature of his wife, feisty, independent, and utterly adorable.

Susannah sighed. "OK." Her lips turned up in a sunny smile. "Can I have my cake with ice cream?"

"Of course you can, precious," Agnes Kincaid said before Ryan could open his mouth. She held out her hand. "You come with Granny, darling. I'll help you wash up and then you can decide if you want vanilla ice cream or if you'd rather pick a different flavor from the freezer."

Ryan got to his feet and sighed dramatically as Agnes whisked his daughter away.

"Grandfather," he said, "you've really met your match."

James chuckled. "That's why I married her, my boy. How could I have let such a gem slip away?"

Ryan smiled and sat down beside the old man. "Bettina's coming for a visit next month," he said quietly.

"Good. We haven't seen her in quite some time."

"No. Not since Jamie was born."

The older man nodded. "Is Devon looking forward to the visit?"

"It was her idea. I don't think they'll ever be close, Grandfather." He smiled slightly. "I mean, this isn't going to turn into anybody's version of a mother-daughter relationship made in heaven, but they've made peace with each other."

James patted Ryan's hand. "I'm happy to hear it, my boy. The older one gets, the more foolish it seems to hold old grudges."

"Hello, everybody."

Ryan, James and Devon all looked around. Frank Ross was standing in the doorway, smiling nervously.

"Frank," Ryan said happily. A grin stretched across his face as he jumped to his feet and hurried toward his oldest friend, his hand outstretched. "I'm glad you could make it, old buddy. How've you..."

Ryan fell silent as a petite, pretty redhead stepped out from behind Frank's bulky shape.

"Hello," she said. "I hope I'm not in the way. I told Frank there was nothing worse than taking an uninvited guest to a party, but he insisted."

There was a silence and then Devon plunked little Jamie into his grandfather's welcoming arms, and rushed forward.

"Of course you're not in the way." Devon held out her hand. "I'm Devon Kincaid. This is my husband, Ryan, his grandfather, James, and that bouncing bundle of energy is our son, Jamie."

The redhead smiled at everybody and took Devon's hand. "I've heard so much about you...

I feel as if I know you all. My name is Sarah. And I'm—I'm—"

"She's my wife," Frank blurted, his face turning a bright red.

Ryan stared at his old friend and then he began to grin.

"You sly old so-and-so! You've been keeping secrets!"

Frank's color deepened. "Yeah, well, I didn't want to say anything until I was sure she would have me."

Sarah made a face. "As if I'd have given him the chance to get away," she said, and gave her husband a smile filled with love. The smile he gave her in return was enough to melt the polar ice caps.

"And then," Frank said, "then, well, we thought we'd announce our engagement and have a wedding in a couple of weeks." He looked at Ryan. "But then I remembered your wedding, well, yours and Devon's, and what a nervous wreck you were…oh, jeez, Devon, I'm sorry. I didn't mean…"

Devon laughed and linked her arm through Sarah's. "Frank's understating it," she said. "We weren't nervous, we were petrified. Come on, let me search out the rest of the crew for introductions and maybe, by the time we get back here for cake and coffee, my husband and your husband will have recovered from their mutual shock."

Ryan waited until the laughing women had disappeared. Then he clapped Frank on the back.

"You finally did it, pal," he said.

Frank blushed. "She's a wonderful girl, Ryan. Wait until you get to know her."

"I'm sure she is. And I'm sure you're going to be very, very happy."

Frank grinned. "Yeah." He looked past Ryan to where James sat, smiling and taking it all in. "Hi, Mr. Kincaid. Happy birthday."

James's smile widened. "Hello, Frank. Congratulations on finally finding a wife."

"Not just a wife, sir. A proper wife."

Ryan laughed, but his laughter faded as he looked across the room.

The kitchen door had opened again and now everyone he loved most in all the world was gathered in this one place. His grandfather, his grandfather's wife, his oldest and dearest friend and his friend's bride, who would surely take her rightful place in this extended family.

His gaze fell on the three special joys of his life. His beautiful, healthy son. His beautiful, healthy daughter...

And Devon.

His throat constricted as his eyes met hers. My wife, he thought, my exquisite, wonderful wife.

The noise and the laughter in the room faded as he went toward her. She smiled up at him as he slipped his arm around her waist and drew her into the kitchen. The door swung shut behind them and Devon laughed breathlessly as he took her into his arms.

"What?" she whispered.

Ryan kissed her. His heart and soul were in the kiss, and she put her arms around him and kissed him back with the same sweet intensity.

"I love you," he said softly, and he smiled and kissed her again and wondered how long it would take Frank to figure out what he and James and every other man who'd ever loved a woman had surely known in their hearts since time began.

There was no such thing as a proper wife.

There was only the one woman in the world whom Fate had created, just for you.

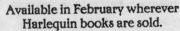

HARLEQUIN PRESENTS®

A new story from one of Harlequin Presents' most
popular authors

#1863 ONE-MAN WOMAN
by
Carole Mortimer

Ellie was only interested in one-to-one relationships,
so Daniel Thackery wasn't for her. But she had
to keep him talking: he seemed to be up to no
good and—even more important—he knew the
whereabouts of her sister's estranged husband.
Only Ellie's persistence seemed to encourage
Daniel to think that she could yet
become his woman!

Available in February wherever
Harlequin books are sold.

Heartbreak RANCH

Four generations of independent women...
Four heartwarming, romantic stories of the West...
Four incredible authors...

Fern Michaels
Jill Marie Landis
Dorsey Kelley
Chelley Kitzmiller

Saddle up with Heartbreak Ranch, an outstanding
Western collection that will take you on a whirlwind
trip through four generations and the exciting,
romantic adventures of four strong women who
have inherited the ranch from Bella Duprey,
famed Barbary Coast madam.

Available in March,
wherever Harlequin books are sold.

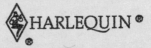

HARLEQUIN ®